*Happy Reading!*

*— Maithili Pradhan*

# Death at Timberly

MAITHILI PRADHAN

To my Dan

# CONTENTS

# ACKNOWLEDGMENTS

Always my first reader and biggest supporter, a huge toodle-pip for my sister Sai. For the most in-depth, honest, and useful advice, a big hug for Deetsy, who was always my intended audience. Without the feedback from my parents Vinita and Prakash, my mother-in-law Joan, and my dear friend Rasika, this book would never have seen the light of day. And without the incredible work of Krista and Dee, it certainly wouldn't have looked so pretty. And finally, of course, a huge thank you to my Dan, without whom this little "project" would not have been possible at all.

# PROLOGUE

"Biff—oh there you are!" Marty Hemming, a plump, charming lady on just the right side of fifty, found her husband frowning over some papers and letters in front of the open French windows in the library. A book on orchids and other hot house plants lay on a carved wooden table nearby. 1930 had not been a successful year for Biff thus far, but at least his orchids were doing well. Marty went over to him, distractedly picking up an ornamental bowl from one of the incidental tables, and depositing it haphazardly on the glass display case of 17th and 18th century snuff boxes. Along with the bowl she left behind a scarf and a flower she had absently picked up elsewhere in the house, and finally came to rest on the arm of her husband's chair.

Used to his wife's vague flowing into and out of rooms after twenty-odd years of marriage, Biff narrowly avoided having Marty scatter his papers over the desk. He wasn't quick enough for the book, however, which she picked up— letting the bookmark drift to the floor, as Biff noted with a sigh—and dropped on to another stool, just out of his reach.

"I'm so worried about this weekend and I can't quite think what's going to happen. Why did Arthur have to pick this weekend to visit, with Julie bringing that young man of hers! Although of course I never would have agreed to Father's scheme of matching up Julie and Arthur. But then, I know Julie was rather sweet on him some months ago and I do think they'd do quite well if only Arthur could forget for an instant that Father wanted them together and kept pushing for it. And all because he's Father's godson and will get a third of his estate. And she's gone and picked a painter! I suppose he's received in all the good houses," Marty continued, dubiously, "but really, I can't quite think Father will be ecstatic about that, do you?"

"I'm sure he'll understand," Biff said soothingly, rescuing the now mangled flower from his wife's hands and returning it to its brethren in a nearby vase.

"Do you really think so Biff?" Marty turned pale, watery eyes toward her husband. "It's just that even I can't quite get myself to approve wholeheartedly, you know, and if he doesn't come from money…well, in any case, I'm sure Julie's worth more than anything Father might ever leave her, but still! Though I must admit Father was right about the last fellow." Marty sighed and gave one of her hands to Biff to pat comfortingly.

"Of course, Arthur *will* make it his business to show this new fellow in the worst light, of that I am convinced. I can't quite tell about him. He didn't want Julie when he could've married her for the asking, but he always seems likely to scotch anyone else she might be interested in. Just like Father in that way."

"It'll be quite alright, dear, don't worry. You're inviting Lucy and Maude, aren't you? Such wonderful girls, they'll make sure Arthur doesn't interfere. You can depend on them!"

"Oh we were lucky to become friends with them, weren't we? To think a horrible Women's Institute breakfast could actually lead to something good! And did I tell you, Biff, Dr. Witting—Harris, you know—called up, and what with one thing and another, I invited him too. I wouldn't say he was angling for it exactly, but I got the feeling he didn't want to be alone while his mother's away. But don't you think dear that he would be just lovely for Maude? She's so spritely, and he's just the sort of calm, stable person she needs in her life."

Biff felt it worthless to protest that the spirited Maude might want someone a bit sharper than the dull doctor, and merely murmured in agreement. He patted Marty's hand again and said, "Don't worry about the weekend. Your father can get quite crusty, but I'm sure he'll warm up to this new fellow of Julie's. And it'll be lovely having Maude and Lucy around."

"And don't you worry either. We'll get father to understand he just has to help you out of this fix. It's not your fault after all, and you couldn't help it if your old business partner took on debts in your name! If only we can get everyone to play nicely, maybe he'll warm up a bit."

Biff's smile faltered a little. "It really isn't right to ask him again, Marty. He's made his views perfectly clear. I'll just have to muddle through this the best I can."

Marty, who had slowly been working from worried distraction to good cheer now grasped Biff's hand with energy. She directed a brilliant smile upon her worried husband and declared, "Don't you worry about a thing, my darling, this weekend is going to be wonderful! It'll work out well for everyone!"

Biff could only smile at his wife's vagaries, and allow her to wipe his frown away with a kiss.

# AN INVITATION

"Lucy! Lucy! There's a darling—do go rustle up some breakfast, would you? Dorcey brought up my tea but it's gone cold and I'm starving like a pack of jackals!"

A curly mop poked over the stairs as Maude Grimsworth, youngest twig of the once abundant and now sadly reduced Chilton Grimsworth family tree, tugged a blue silk robe around her slim frame as the sash trailed off behind her, making her petite figure even more diminutive than usual. The dark hair, which at this moment took the form of a fluffy thatch rather than their usual ordered curls, framed a creamy complexion, high cheek bones, and a pair of large blue-grey eyes. These eyes were a little too large, the chin a little too firm, and the jaw a little too set to be called pretty. Striking, rather than beautiful, the face was now screwed up preparatory to a loud yell.

"Lucy!"

"Darling, you've scared poor Jacko again! Do stop your bawling! Now I'll have to spend an hour coaxing him out from behind my grandmother's favorite chair, and I'm sure he'll put a few more scratches in it just out of spite."

"Spite! I'll spite him! Why you keep that dratted creature in this home of love and warmth I'll never know. Just because he was born to the family cat! We should leave him to fend for himself among all the barn cats. See how he makes out with creatures who can claw him right back!"

"A mouser, darling! And after they drowned all of his siblings, I couldn't bear to leave the poor thing. He used to be such a sweet kitten. I know he seems rather to have left the

4

adorable kittenliness behind, but he would never survive out there now! He's a proper old house cat, poor fellow."

Lucy Belling, a fair-haired, sturdy, and thoroughly capable young damsel, laughed and shook her head at Maude as she gazed up at her from the hall. It had been a happy day when she had thought of inviting Maude to come stay with her and play the role of companion. Lucy had been orphaned for a second time when her much older brother James had died a few years ago. After boarding school (where she and Maude had, much to their relief, found kindred souls in each other) and a stint with her Aunt Delilah (during which she was unsuccessful in obediently finding a good husband), Lucy had decided twenty-one was as good an age as any to seize her independence and set herself up at the family manse. It was the end of the '20s and perfectly acceptable, she had told her aunt, for two young women to set up house for themselves without outdated chaperones. And she had the perfect companion in mind.

When Lucy had invited Maude to join her in what she termed a "delightful adventure with Dorcey to take care of us," Maude had been only too eager to say yes. She had been left bereft at the end of the war when her father had succumbed to the pain of losing both sons before changing his will and providing more than a modest inheritance for his only daughter. His estate—or at least what little there was left of it after the ravages of the war and the death duties—had devolved to a third cousin who was only too happy to inherit a house with enough space for his brood of six extremely energetic young children. After months of living with this kindly but boisterous family, the prospect of living with a dear friend and with some peace and quiet meant that the very next day Maude had packed her bags and undertaken the three transfers to Bellingsley, a beautiful Kentish estate spilling over into the northern tip of East Sussex.

Thankfully for Lucy, the estate manager had kept the farms in thriving condition. She was dependent on the estate's profits for her income, although supplemented to some extent by the fanciful stories she secretly wrote under the pen name of Pyloria Braithwaite. The adventures and romantic follies of her heroine, the Hon. Holly Galbraith, had a staunch following, but Lucy was glad the estate didn't depend on the meager sums her publisher paid her every month. The enormous mansion, unlike the estate, had been allowed to fall into a state of dereliction. And so Lucy, Maude, Dorcey and, to Maude's great dissatisfaction, Jacko (who had long outgrown any mythical sweet kittenliness), had moved into the dowager house—a sunny, cheerful little abode, which was eminently more suited to two self-sufficient young women and a cook/housekeeper with an aching knee. With the laudable goal of refurbishing the grand house and creating a life for themselves, they had settled into a pleasant mode of life, keeping themselves busy with work and social engagements.

"Blast that mouser. I'd prefer a couple of sweet brown mice than that howling, hissing little hellion. Do go see what Dorcey's up to, will you? Like I said, jackals couldn't be hungrier than me—than I—than me—blast, whichever! And I'll be down in two shakes of a duck's tail." Maude whirled away from the stairs as Lucy turned to seek out Dorcey and then, if he was in an amenable mood, to coax Jacko out into the open again.

\*

Curls now bouncing glossily about, Maude had made short work of a stack of toast and a mound of scrambled eggs. With a wide awake and satisfied smile, she reached out for her letters. She and Lucy were sitting having their daily gossip in the morning room. Furnished for comfort rather than aesthetic, this and the little library were their preferred nests. The favorite pieces of past generations of Bellings, ranging from a side table of unknown Jacobite origin to a tall Victorian whatnot and a fine Sheraton secretaire were collected here in a jumbling, comfortable way. Cheerful daisies in a tall, thin vase sat on a side table. The curtains were a sunny yellow, and the cerulean sofa and chair—sadly a bit scratched about the legs due to Jacko's vindictive nature—were approaching a state of well-loved shabbiness.

"We have the shooting party at Glow-worm's in a few weeks, but nothing before that, is there?"

"How you can! Poor Gloria. Whatever did she do to have that appalling nickname bestowed upon her?!" Lucy quirked her eyebrows, wondering how Maude always seemed to blurt out the first thing on her mind.

"Oh she doesn't mind. It slipped out once when I was with her, but I just told her it was because she always has such a nice glow about her. But to be honest, it was more because when we were fourteen she always had the shiniest, most glowingest little nose you ever did see! In fact, she—"

Maude paused as the shrill tones of the telephone sounded through the house. She uncoiled her legs from underneath her orange patterned skirt and went into the hall, where the telephone occupied a place of honor.

As Lucy returned to her own letters, she heard bits and pieces of a one-sided conversation, from which she gathered that their friend Marty had called about something wonderful that the two of them would be absolutely delighted about. She held her peace, however, reflecting that Maude was unlikely to volunteer their services for something excruciating like a Women's Institute talk or something—they had both sworn the one and only talk they had ever attended would be their last—and hoped it was something a bit more pleasant. Tea in town or a little shopping in London perhaps. She was sure Marty could use a break from her tyrant of a father, and perhaps Biff could be persuaded to join them as well.

A few minutes later Maude skipped back into the morning room exclaiming, "Luce! We are to be social butterflies! Glow-worm's party is merely one of our many social engagements, my dear! We are, as they say, in high demand!"

"Was that Marty? Has she asked us to tea or something? It's a bit of a trek to get out there, but it would be lovely to see them both!"

"Even better! She's asked us to come up this Thursday for a few days for a house party! Although," Maude said, her smile fading a little, "Marty's inviting us to serve as buffers rather than as charming houseguests. Julie—Marty's niece, we met her last summer—is coming up and bringing her young man to get Reginald's approval this weekend. Not promising because ol' Reginald wants his granddaughter to marry slinky godson Arthur Pendleton—although why, I can't fathom. I know there was something between the two at some point, but from whatever Marty's said recently you wouldn't think they could bear to be in the same room together. I suppose Reginald likes the idea because Arthur's the only man on this mortal coil that he tolerates. Likes, even! Marty thought it'd be a good idea to invite the two—Julie and her fellow, that is—up for the weekend so Reginald could get to know the chappie and see he's not a bounder or anything. But Arthur invited himself up this very weekend too!"

As Arthur had once or twice shown up Marty in a bad light for not having her domestics in order, the poor scatterbrain. Lucy couldn't bring herself to express joy at this announcement. Seeing her face, Maude went on with the air of one unshrinkingly fair and just, "He's funny in his own way. Got that dry sort of air about him, and always dressed just so. One must appreciate those points. In any case, Arthur *will* poke at everything, and I'm sure Marty, poor soul, will be harassed to death! So we're to be decoys or screens or what-have-yous."

"Phew! In any case, it'll be lovely to see Marty and Biff. It's been ages. And I can't say I blame her for wanting to provide a bit of a buffer. It'll be nice for them to have our kindly souls around, and it'll be good to get a bit away from civilization—such as it is here—for a few days, even if Marty's father will be around to make sure nobody laughs too much."

"Yes, Reginald is a cantankerous old blight isn't he? Always down on everybody." Maude cheerfully disposed of his character and turned to another letter.

Lucy rolled her eyes at Maude. Her friend was a bit too forthright, and perhaps prone to a little exaggeration, but of course she had hit the nail right on the head. Lord Reginald Timberly, Marty's father, had refilled the slightly empty family coffers through a number of nefarious deals. Nobody was quite sure how he had made his money, but it was well-known there were pots of it, if only Reginald could be induced to loosen his clutched fist a little. Biff and Marty (more officially Lord Bartholomew and Lady Hemming), lived with Reginald because he needed somebody to keep house for him without having to be paid and because Biff, with the best of intentions and the worst of luck, was the opposite of Reginald when it came to business sense. Where Reginald, with his shiny bald pate, fierce snapping eyes and lowering brows, would have stabbed his partner in the back to get one extra groat, Biff, a gentle, mild-mannered soul of middling age with wavy brown hair and large doe-eyes, would happily sign over his share to help a friend in need. When gout and age had inspired Reginald to bid Marty and Biff come stay at Timberly, the two had moved in, having just lost the house where they had spent twenty happy years together and where they had welcomed Marty's orphaned niece, Julie, for her summers home from the vastly refined Miss Pritchett's boarding school. Their life at Timberly was overall quite comfortable if one could only dismiss Reginald's bursts of temper, his riding roughshod over Marty, his disdainful dismissal of Biff, and his threats to write Marty and Julie out of his will.

"Well, I suppose that's true enough," Lucy admitted. "Oh dear! I thought we were in for a pleasant weekend, but it sounds rather like a game of chess! I wonder what Julie's like now. We only saw her once last summer, didn't we? Seemed like a decent kid, though a bit too conscious of her own worth, don't you think? Has that terribly lazy way of speaking too, as though the words just weren't worth the effort. Any other guests sure to bring disaster to this charming house party?"

"Well, I rather think Marty meant it as a peace offering to me, since she's inviting us as buffers for herself, but it's rather ghastly. Harris Witting!"

"Harris! Oh no! But darling, he isn't really all that bad, is he?"

"But he moons, Luce! He moons! Always and forever mooning here and mooning there. Blasted Harris Witting."

"Oh darling, but I think he does love you! And I believe he's come into some money recently."

"Love! Faugh! He's a silly nutter and I don't think he even knows what real love is. Besides, I've always thought there isn't something quite right about him, even if he *is* a doctor." Maude screwed up her face in distaste. "He only thinks he loves me because I had tea with his mother and she took a liking to me, and he likes whatever his mother likes. And even if he's inherited some money, just think! Dr. Harris Witting! The man doesn't like reading anything apart from his anatomical books!"

"I know he's a bit much, sometimes, but I suppose Marty thinks it's sweet. It is a bit of a pain, though, you'll have to avoid him."

"Lest he think I'm encouraging him!"

"You could, of course, use some of that forthright manner you seem to cultivate and use it to tell the poor man he's got no chance!"

Maude's brows lowered, and her eyes turned a deeper shade of grey as she contemplated Dr. Witting. "But I can't, Luce! Oh lawd, don't you remember what a fool he made of himself when I danced with him at the Appleton's ball and tried to tell him it was a no-go? I thought I would never get him to stop dropping by looking like a dying puppy. No. I'll just have to hope he falls in love with someone else. Or better yet, falls in a well!" With a dramatic wave of her hand, Maude declared: "Luce, isn't it enough that we are to be martyrs upon the altar of friendship?! We'll be trying to avoid Harris and promote Julie and her young man and helping to buffer

Marty from Reginald's outbursts and I'm sure Arthur's likely to be difficult too, even if he does make one laugh sometimes. It can't be done!"

Lucy let out a sudden trilling laugh, sweet and infectious in quality, at Maude's pose. "Oh Maudie! We'll have fun, don't worry! It will be interesting at least, and we needn't be bored while waiting for Glow-worm's party! Come now, there's a dear!" In a twinkling Maude's face went from a moue of displeasure to a bright chuckle. The usually staid and restful Lucy always had this effect on her when she started laughing.

"Let's have some fun, Luce! What shall we pack? Dorcey! Dorcey! Come help us pack and bring us some snacks to sustain us while we do it!"

# ARRIVAL AT TIMBERLY

The old Daimler was covered in dust by the time it finally turned off what was deceptively called the main road but might have been better described as a dirt path according to Marsh, who had been chauffeur at Bellingsley for over twenty years and therefore was not at all shy about expressing his opinion to his employer. He heaved a sigh of relief and thanked his stars that Miss Lucy and Miss Maude usually preferred to have Lady Hemming visit them at Bellingsley instead of having him drive them out to the only part of Surrey that still remained desolate, neglected by the many railroads that seemed to otherwise criss-cross the county, and by all the actual main roads as well. The car turned in through the massive wrought iron gates and went up the curving drive lined with stately oaks. As the gravel drive swept around a curve they crested the little hill and saw Timberly Hall rising up to greet them. The large house still showed the bones of its medieval origins but had been expanded upon by a succession of Timberlys with little regard for uniformity. The end result was not unpleasing to the eye, but could not be said to look overly welcoming. A slightly straggly, yellowing lawn fronted the house, and the parkland surrounding the Hall was set off by a thickly wooded slope in the back. At this hour between lunch and tea, the estate was quiet. The oppressive heat and haze seemed to press down on the house, giving the entire thing a slightly jaundiced appearance. Only a couple of cheerful rose bushes planted near the entrance at Biff's direction lightened the somber aspect.

The car rolled to a stop and, flinging the doors open

without waiting for Marsh to decorously open them, Maude and Lucy made their way up the stairs, straightening their crumpled traveling skirts and shaking out their legs in most unladylike fashion. A tall, thin, grey-haired crow opened the imposing doors.

"Hallo, Jennings!" Maude and Lucy exclaimed.

The dour faced butler raised one corner of his mouth in welcome. This was an honor reserved for the select few, and Miss Grimsworth and Miss Belling were the top favorites, the one flighty and irrepressible, the other calm and sensible.

As he bowed them in, a vision of plump comfort and softness descended upon Maude and Lucy, batting away wisps of mousey blonde hair that had, as usual, come undone. "Darlings! You're here! My saviors!" Marty quickly glanced around, but spying nobody other than the trustworthy Jennings, gave a guilty smile and flapped on, "Jennings will take care of all your things. I'm sure your Marsh knows exactly where to stow the car and what to do with your bags and belongings, and more than likely he's already on his way to the kitchen to get a cup of tea with Mrs. Basset, but you must come with me, darlings, for I have to introduce you to Garth, who is—well, he's Julie's young man, so we must make the most of it. Come, come!"

And with a whirl of scarves and embraces, Maude and Lucy found themselves being energetically herded along to a pleasant sitting room decorated in shades of straw and cool green. As soon as they were seated in a couple of comfortable wingback chairs by the empty fireplace, Marty launched into a rather convoluted monologue. People getting cut out of wills, snakes (used as an adjective, Lucy hoped, as she surreptitiously raised her ankles an inch above the floor) with no proper family feeling, and old business deals seemed to figure largely. Maude tried to interrupt here and there to catch the thread of the story, but it was Lucy who, sitting quietly, thought she actually understood what Marty was rattling on about. From what she could gather, Reginald was in a more infernal temper than usual, even snapping at the unfortunate

Dr. Harris Witting. Some old business deal of Biff's had turned up to haunt him, and there was something about the roof in the west wing, to boot. Lucy heartily hoped she and Maude had rooms as far from the west wing as possible. They had seen heavy clouds advancing upon Timberly during their drive, and she didn't think having a leak in her bedroom would add to the pleasure of the weekend.

Finally Maude laughingly pulled her hostess down to sit next to herself on the settee, saying "Do stop, Marty! The ride's been ghastly longish and we're not quite ready for all this runaway conversation just yet!"

With a final flustered sigh and a little chuckle, Marty sat down and pushed a strand of hair behind her ear. "I am rather a clucking hen, aren't I? I've been trying to soothe Julie and it's made me jittery instead! Perhaps I didn't do a good job of it. But I really can't think that Garth is quite right! But never mind that. I'm so relieved to see you both. I have high hopes you'll make the whole thing go off between the two of you, and I will be so grateful! But how was the drive, dears?"

"Not quite as terrible as Maude would have you believe," Lucy said as she took off her straw hat trimmed with a jaunty little feather. "Just a rotten tire while we were furthest away from civilization. But I must admit, I'd like to get freshened up before you start introducing us to all your guests!"

"You're right, my dear, you're right. You both shall go to your rooms, rest and refresh, and I'll have Mrs. Basset send up some lemonade for you. Tea is in an hour out on the terrace—it's rather a muggy afternoon isn't it? I thought maybe if there's a breeze it might be tolerable. I just hope the rain holds off. Just my luck, we'll all be stuck inside all weekend and everything will go to hell in a handbag!"

*

"Come in!"

The handle turned, and Lucy stepped into Maude's bedroom—a dark apartment, whose stone floors and wood paneling preserved what coolness they could, but did little to really relieve the oppressive heat. She had changed from her traveling suit into a pale green cotton dress with flared cap sleeves and cinched at the waist to give her straight figure a more feminine touch. The dress flowed down to skim her calves and contrasted nicely with her liquid brown eyes.

"Lawd! Marty's a mess, isn't she?" Maude called from the vanity, where she was struggling to clasp a delicate gold band around her wrist.

"Here, let me help you with that, you little goose. You've got it on backwards! Yes, I wonder what's happened to send dear Marty into one of her spirals? She's not usually quite as batty as all that!"

"Most of it must be because of Reginald, ghastly man. But I'm sure you'll find out what's what soon enough. People do rather make it a habit of confiding in you." Maude directed a darkling look at Lucy and said aggrievedly, "Little do they know you're only going to make them the subject of some sharp, witty little story, Madam Pyloria Brai—"

"Maude!" Of course, it was true the esteemed Miss Pyloria Braithwaite's last story had included a flibbertigibbety character that might, in some circumstances, have borne some slight hint of resemblance to Maude, but it had been completely unintentional and almost flattering, really, in the right light, as Lucy had hastened to assure her dear friend.

"Alright, alright, I know I promised, even if I'm being slandered and libeled right and left. Anyway, I'm glad Marty put you next to me. She was so flustered when she posted me in here, I was sure she'd lead you to the rafters!"

"I think we're the only ones at this end of the hall, close to the front stairs. Julie, Harris, Arthur, and of course, Biff and Marty, are on the other side. Garth, poor thing, is up on the next floor! Apparently Reginald insisted that—what did Marty say he called the poor chap?—oh, that the 'lugabout' couldn't have any of the best bedrooms, which are all on this floor. The only other rooms on this side seem to be Reginald's apartments—I saw his man go into those massive doors catty corner from ours, just by the stairs."

"Oh good. It means you and I are the only ones sharing the bathroom on this end then. And it's probably a good thing everyone else is on the other end, so we won't hear Harris Witting stomping around as he does!"

"Oh you and Harris. You've taken a proper dislike to him, and the poor doctor just loves you! But," Lucy hurriedly went on, as she saw Maude's brows lower, "you're right, of course. And if you're quite done fiddling with that bracelet, down we go. I'm dying for a nice cup of tea, but even more, I'm dying to find out who all these characters are that Marty's gathered for the weekend!"

# TEA AND TENSION

The two stepped out on to the terrace into a thick wave of humidity. Even Maude, who had looked crisp and cool in a becoming dress of rose pink, stopped to mop little beads of perspiration from her nose. A fair, rather bovine young giant turned to take in the vision of the two lively and smiling girls chattering good humoredly and seeming to lighten the muggy atmosphere a bit. The middle-aged man he had been speaking to turned as well, and his slightly doughy face creased into a smile of pleasure.

"Maude, Lucy! So lovely to see you both again—it's been an age, hasn't it?" Biff stooped to kiss both the girls on the cheek and made way for Harris Witting to greet them too.

"Hallo, Biff, darling. How are you?" Maude turned to smile a little stiffly at the doctor, who was gazing at her with a too-wide smile on his face. Lucy, unencumbered by not being the object of his affection, said a cordial hello and started chatting about their drive down to Timberly, drawing Harris apart from Biff and Maude.

As the four shifted into duos, Marty arrived, complaining about the gardener, who refused to go down to his shed to retrieve rat poison for Mrs. Basset on account of his knee, which foretold rain in the near future. Biff kissed his wife's cheek and kindly helped her extract herself from one of the scarves that seemed in danger of strangling her. He mildly protested, "Rat poison in the house? Surely there has to be a better way than that..."

"Oh Biff, with vermin you have to be downright unscrupulous," Marty exclaimed. "Once you let a rat get its

17

own way, you're done for. Better to get in there and do the job quickly." Marty was transformed into a steely-eyed killer as she clenched her fists and waved them at imaginary rats. Maude and Lucy exchanged glances and had to turn away from each other to stifle snorts of laughter at this sudden vision of Maude as a lethal murderer—aided and abetted by Biff and the kindly housekeeper, Mrs. Basset, no less! Harris did not seemed to have heard and continued talking to Lucy ponderously about his practice. He was lucky most of his patients were generous, he said, because of the tough times.

"Well, if it must be done, I don't quite see why Groby needs to come into it, my dear. Let the poor chap rest his arthritic knees. Surely Mrs. Basset can get some from the conservatory? I know there's a tin in there. On the shelves below the orchid at the back."

"Biff! You're a genius! I never even thought of it! The Basset will just have to sniff out the poison for herself then! One only hopes she won't drop some in the soup as well, though I'm sure I can think of a few who deserve it here," Marty muttered darkly.

As they had been speaking, two figures had rounded the corner of the house and stepped onto the porch. The tall, slender girl mopped her brow delicately with her handkerchief, waving her hand at everyone dispiritedly. As Lucy and Maude started to greet her, Julie leaned forward to kiss the air next to their cheeks. "Too hot to be groping about, darlings," she said in an indifferent tone. "If I hadn't wanted to get as far away from Grandpapa as I could, I would never have taken that walk. It's no cooler down by the lake either. We should be having iced lemonade instead of tea." She turned to the lanky young man who had accompanied her and was now greeting Harris and Biff. "Sweetums, would you go hurry along Jennings and see where tea is? I couldn't eat a bite, but I am rather dying of thirst you know."

Lucy's ears pricked up and Maude's left eyebrow rose involuntarily at this form of address. They waited with bated breath to see how "Sweetums" would respond. Both were sorely disappointed when he merely smiled at Julie and turned to pause disconcertedly in front of them. Feeling rather sorry for the fellow, the two girls smiled at him helpfully. Julie waved a languid hand, saying, "Oh meet Maude and Lucy, would you. They're awfully darling and live just down the way—or as down the way as you can from this isolated outpost!"

The two darling damsels politely extended their hands in greeting. Barely touching their hands, the young man nodded a few times and spoke, a little too quickly, "Garth. A pleasure and a delight to meet you. Julie has been telling me about you, of course, and I've been waiting to make your acquaintance. It's so nice to meet Julie's friends." And turning to Lucy, "Amazing what you're doing, Miss Belling—a single female, taking on the task, a mission really, and a noble mission at that—of restoring a grand house, and after facing such a loss. I would like to offer some words of comfort or wisdom, but alas, what comfort can a stranger offer in a time of such sorrow? As a painter I understand exactly how you feel—the artistic imagination, you know, is strong in me—and you can take some comfort in that at least."

Repressing a strong urge to snap the fellow's nose off at bringing up matters liable to put her out of all countenance, Lucy mumbled something polite and, feeling a telltale red creeping up her neck and a pricking behind her eyes, quickly turned around to greet a smooth faced young man who had entered from the house at the same time Julie and Garth had rounded the corner. Arthur might be a bit of a bounder where Marty was concerned, but at least he wouldn't wax poetic about her "noble mission," nor would he bring up her brother's death in casual conversation at first hello.

"Hello, Arthur. How nice to see you here!"

"Hello Lucy. I would say the pleasure is all mine, but perhaps I have been outjockeyed already," he said with a sardonic yet not quite unkind smile, bending over Lucy's outstretched hand with a theatrical flourish and an understanding smirk in his eyes. Annoyed that he should so clearly sense her discomfort, yet grateful for the joking note in his voice, Lucy smiled a trifle awkwardly. She was saved from having to make a reply by Maude, who joined the two in an effort to get away from Harris. Only moments later, however, the doctor's ponderous tread approached. Harris, distrustful of Arthur's charm, made his presence felt. Arthur's smile grew even wider at this audience, and he proceeded to subject Maude to a full assault of flirtatious nonsense. As Lucy suppressed her quiet laughter and tried unsuccessfully to draw the doctor's attention away, Maude responded with some gusto, if only to combat Harris' scowls and show him just how ridiculous his possessiveness was. Lucy caught a wicked glint in Arthur's eye that showed just how much of the situation he understood, and had to turn away to hide a chuckle.

As the little group had been gathering on the terrace, the atmosphere had slowly darkened. Only a half hour ago the sun had been blazing steamily on a hazy, humid, day. Now, pendulous, heavy bottomed clouds were rolling in. Jennings opened the French doors leading on to the terrace and a thunder clap echoed in the far distance as though to mark the entrance of the tea tray. He deposited the tea things on a spindly engraved table that looked as though it might give up the ghost at any moment. Going back toward the door leading into the drawing room, he held it open for Lord Reginald Timberly. His lordship entered on a note of grumbling fit to match that of the thunder roiling a few miles away.

"Tea on the terrace. Always something new whenever guests are over, upsetting my stomach and going to bring on a flare of my gout again, I'll wager. Ho! There you are, eh, Marty. Let's not stand gawping about, my girl, I've had to drag myself out onto the terrace and I'm parched. Or have you pulled us all out here to stare at each other?"

Visibly distressed, Marty hurried over to the table and started pouring the tea and handing out delicate china cups.

Maude made a grim face at Lucy and stepped toward Reginald to fulfill her duties as a screen against Reginald's already exacerbated temper. After a few moments she had succeeded in getting Reginald to crack a smile—he did enjoy being flattered by pretty young things after all, and Maude's effervescence suited him exactly, although the same impulsiveness in any less young or personable female would be deemed frivolous. Finding in her a fellow non-admirer of the doctor, he entered into a good mood and embarked on several highly colored anecdotes. So successful was Maude at laughing at the right moments that he was well on his way to almost becoming almost jolly. However, just as he was about to launch into another story, Arthur approached with a cup of tea for his godfather and destroyed the upward tick in Reginald's mood that Maude had so carefully cultivated.

"For you, Uncle Reg. Unfortunately Marty doesn't have the almond seed cake you prefer, but shall I fetch you a sandwich instead?" Reginald's brows lowered again and he started a diatribe about Marty's poor management.

As another crack of thunder sounded—much closer, this time—he spied Julie and Garth sitting on the far side of the terrace, partially hidden by a wilting aspidistra. "Ho! There you are, eh? And that fellow's still hanging about you! No word of hello for your own grandfather, is it!"

Julie rose slowly and walked over to bestow a cool half-kiss on the wrinkled cheek. As she was about to turn away, Reginald grasped her wrist and held her there with surprising strength.

"You won't do it, you know, if I have anything to say to it!"

"A pity you don't then," said Julie, her mounting color belying her supercilious tone.

"Ho! And how do you think you'll buy your pretty gowns and gew-gaws when I've stopped your allowance and cut you off, eh? Think that ninny'll set you up? You've got another think coming! And don't think your silly Aunt Marty or that useless Biff will have anything to say to it either! In fact I have a good mind to call Jellaby and tell him to get up here!"

Julie's eyes flashed dangerously, and she looked like she was about to make a retort, but Garth had shuffled over as though attached to her by a leash, and bumbled in, "Why hello, sir, what a pleasure to see you again this afternoon. Julie, darling, would you like another cup of tea?"

Julie disentangled her wrist from Reginald's grasp with a sharp tug and turned away with Garth. Maude, still sitting awkwardly next to her glowering host, wildly grasped for the first person who came to mind, blurting out, "Biff was telling me—"

Thankfully, considering Reginald's brows had descended even further upon hearing Biff's name, she never got to say what Biff was telling her. It occurred to Maude that during their brief friendship with the Hemmings, she and Lucy had never quite got a handle on how Reginald and Biff got along. Typically Reginald at least seemed to tolerate Biff, but this afternoon it appeared that Biff was most definitely a *persona non grata*. At that very moment the sky, which had rapidly gone from a musty blue to a deep velvety purple, lit up with an arc of lightning stretching from end to end. Only a second or two later, an ear-splitting crash of thunder resounded just around the corner. The roiling black-purple clouds seemed to hold for a moment until, with the sound of a crashing waterfall, they opened to dash a veritable sheet of water around the roofed-in terrace. Everyone jumped up except Reginald, as though this showing of nature's power was worthy of a standing ovation. Arthur, who had been closest to the siding, sprang back nimbly as the rain sprayed in.

"Biff! The ditch! Oh Groby was right, we should've insisted the men finish filling it in or at least cover it or something!" Marty wrung her hands together, dropping a scarf as she did so, and getting her fingers tangled in the rope of beads around her neck.

"No amount of filling in or covering up would stand this, my dear. Let's hope it's only a summer storm that passes quickly, and perhaps it won't quite get flooded."

"Ho! That ditch! Maybe I'll finally have a moat, but more's the pity I'd be stuck inside with the lot of you!" That was Reginald, of course.

"A moat, darling? Are we to be flooded in, do you suppose?" Lucy whispered to Marty.

"Oh I don't know, father had this idea of digging a moat—always creates such floods, you know. The men have started to fill it in, but only just started. And now it'll get waterlogged and flooded again!" Marty replied, gripping her tea cup so tightly that Lucy half-expected the delicate china to shatter in her fingers.

"Well, delightful as this tea party is, I propose to go inside a bit. All this lightning is giving me a headache," muttered Julie, placing her hand upon Garth's arm and turning away from the group. She paused as she came to where Marty was sitting and bent to give her a fleeting kiss. She murmured in something far different from her usual languid tones, "I'll see you at cocktails, darling. Don't get too fussed, will you?" And exchanging a sweet smile with the aunt who had played mother her entire life, strolled away into the dark interior of the house.

Maude, glancing at Marty, surprised a strikingly tender look on her face. Behind her, Biff slipped off the porch and followed Julie, stopping her a little way inside, holding her hand and nodding his head earnestly, turning around to bestow a look of utter dislike upon Reginald. "If looks could kill!" Maude muttered to herself, and rose to join Lucy on the far side of the terrace where she sat chatting amiably with Arthur.

As Maude perched on a cane chair beside her, Lucy muttered *sotto voce*, "The thunder and lightning in here are more than a match for what Mother Nature's putting on out there!" Giving a wistful sigh she continued, "Atmosphere! If only I had my notebook!"

"Well, so long as we get through this weekend without a murder—though it seems all too likely, doesn't it?"

"I certainly hope not." Lucy rolled her eyes. In a fair

approximation of Julie's affected voice, she said, "I thought I was the imaginative one! Too utterly utter, darling! Where *do* you get these notions?" and held her hand out to let the torrential rain splash on her fingertips.

# DINNER AND DISSENSION

At a little past seven thirty that evening, Biff, Marty, Lucy, and Maude traipsed into the drawing room one after another. Maude was pleased to see a fire crackling merrily in the hearth. Despite its vastness, the room appeared cozy with the curtains drawn against the battle raging in the skies outside. The rain had continued lashing against the windows. Where before there had been a muggy heat pressing in, there was now a distinct bite in the air. Maude was almost regretting wearing a rather daring backless gown. She had loved the bold pattern and thought it would set off her striking features, but hadn't bargained on the sudden summer chill.

Lucy walked over to the fireplace with Maude, but stood a few steps away. Not having chosen a backless gown herself, she didn't feel the need to stand as close to the flames as Maude apparently did. Turning around, Lucy saw the room had filled up and almost everyone had a cocktail in hand. Her eyes came to rest on Garth, wearing a suit that seemed a bit shiny about the shoulders, advancing with a cocktail held with great purpose. He had an air of having girded his loins. As she wondered whether to cut in and save him from the inevitable rebuff—Reginald only drank sherry before dinner and abhorred cocktails—a dry voice behind her said "Don't bother, my dear. Although the impulse is noble, think of the greater good!"

Turning quickly, she faced Arthur and said tartly, "Cruelty to animals, don't you think?"

"Not at all! I was merely suggesting that perhaps it might be better for us all if you let things play out as they must."

As she heard Reginald growl at Garth behind them, Lucy said with some asperity, "Better for us all or merely for you?" Arthur bowed mockingly and responded with some humor, "Touché, my pet, touché! May I offer you a drink? I hope it won't be met with the same treatment as our bashful—and yet, a little slippery, don't you think—friend there."

Although Lucy disliked his attitude, she couldn't bring herself to deny his sharp assessment of Garth and merely said "Yes, thank you."

Arthur stepped away with the hint of a smile, leaving Lucy to look after his precisely turned out figure wavering between annoyance and like-minded sympathy.

Meanwhile, Maude turned around and spied Harris entering the drawing room. As she was assiduously avoiding him, she hurriedly dragged Lucy over toward Biff. He and Julie were seated on the plump Chesterfield sofa in the middle of the room and welcomed the two into a conversation about the latest West End plays. Minutes later, Arthur returned with Lucy's drink and in a few short moments, Julie and he subtly drew a little apart.

"Your ardent admirer seems to be pulling out all the stops, my dear. I shouldn't wonder that he's carried you off, should I? You'll cut Marty and me out altogether!"

Julie's eyes snapped angrily, and she replied in a little more heat than her usual insipid tones, "And so what? Or are you going to pretend you're in love with me now?"

"My dear you wrong me! I should never underestimate you so!"

"Garth loves me!"

Arthur only bowed maliciously and said softly, "Just as well, then, isn't it?" and turned away before Julie, eyes bright and hard as diamonds, could utter a word. He strolled over to Reginald and offered him a cigarette, and both men seemed to share a momentary bond as they turned the conversation away from Garth and, by dint of not quite politely ignoring the unfortunate painter, succeeded in getting him to wander off irresolutely in Marty's direction.

"Got a rather interesting liqueur you might be interested in, sir. Have you come across Fernet?"

"You're no better than the rest of them, but I'll give you this much, you have more palatable taste than most of these gumptionless lugabouts. That young snake there was trying to offer me one of these cocktails! Faugh! Fernet, eh? I haven't tasted that particular poison in years. Come up after dinner and we'll have a sip."

"With pleasure, sir."

"I should warn you, my boy, I've called Jellaby today. Can't have that silly little doll running off with a no-good bounder who's out to get my money. I'd like to see you two make a match of it, and I shall. Going to tie it all up right and tight, and Marty can just hold her own. High time Biff started supporting her!"

Only a slight twitch at the corner of his mouth betrayed Arthur's displeasure at having his matters—and his inheritance—arranged in this imperious way. Giving no other outward sign of annoyance, he merely smiled politely and said, "Your matters are your concern, sir, I should never presume to tell you how to arrange your own affairs."

Reginald darted a sharp, knowing look at Arthur, but decided against asking any questions. He liked Arthur for being able to stand up to him, but damn it all, it was his money, his granddaughter, and his godson; he'd see things arranged as he pleased.

Biff, Lucy, and Maude, standing near enough to hear bits and pieces, acted with one accord and valiantly started discussing the weather, looking up with relief when Jennings arrived to announce dinner. As Biff escorted Julie in, he leaned close and murmured in her ear, in response to which Julie's back became rigid and she turned to bestow an especially warm smile on Garth, and a particularly cold look on Reginald.

The dining room was a large apartment filled with a suitably sized table that promised to discourage any but the most determined conversationalists. A large silver epergne with a multitude of branches and bowls and baskets occupied the center of the table, and crystal glasses and polished silver winked from each place setting. Whatever Marty's failings in the home management business, she had been fortunate in her domestic help. Jennings never failed to put on a good presentation for dinner, nor did Cook ever send forward a dish that was anything less than delectable.

Despite the multitude of delicious courses, the meal itself was thoroughly uncomfortable. Reginald found fault with everything from the soup to the savory, which caused Marty's hair to fall down one side of her face as she kept patting it nervously. He spoke at length of the untrustworthiness of today's generation who were ready to stab their own benefactors in the back. This, aimed rather confusingly at Harris, had the effect of making the stolid doctor turn absolutely dumb. Reginald then went on to utter cryptic remarks about young people in his day listening to their elders and betters, at which Julie and Arthur, in a moment of understanding, exchanged unamused glances. Finally he presented a monologue on the value of having gumption enough to stand up for oneself, in response to which Biff seemed to sink lower in his chair and Garth, already rather pink, turned a deep and even more unbecoming shade of crimson.

Biff was quieter than usual, sending harassed looks between his father-in-law, his wife, and his niece. He had succeeded in aggravating Reginald even further when he fumbled and upset Reginald's glass. He hurriedly proffered his own glass of wine with which he had been toying, and was met with a "faugh!" as Reginald drank a huge gulp and proceeded to denounce the wine with great rancour as well. Garth spilled his soup and scattered breadcrumbs all around his plate in response to Reginald's gruff commentary. Julie's eyes flashed and her voice became lazier than ever. She seemed to pick the subjects most likely to instigate an outburst from her grandfather. Arthur grew steadily more urbane, and Marty turned into an absolute mess. Harris plodded through the courses without saying a word, occasionally sliding bovine but belligerent looks toward Reginald. Maude and Lucy were left to carry the conversation as politely as they could without any assistance from the rest of the table. Although they persevered gamely, eventually they too fell into an awkward silence. This silence hung heavy until the ladies rose to leave and Reginald, disclaiming any desire to have the male company present waste his port, led all the men out with the ladies despite his own old-fashioned beliefs of etiquette.

The drawing room seemed to have lost all its previous coziness. Lucy saw that Julie seemed to be trying to make amends. Perhaps she had felt the wisdom of Biff's warnings about Jellaby's arrival the day after. Indeed, she and Harris almost got into an argument over who would take Reginald's cup to him. Lucy, observing part of this droll exchange, was moved to murmur to herself only a little maliciously, "The princess or the beast—who shall carry the day?"

As it turned out, the princess won this battle, took the cup from Harris, and went off toward Reginald. Harris shuffled his shoulders a little and turned back to receive his own cup. Lucy wondered why he had ever offered to take the coffee to Reginald anyway. The old man had been anything but pleasant to the young doctor all evening.

Marty was bristling a little as she handed out coffee cups. Biff, with some notion of soothing things over, had tried to off-handedly mention Reginald's comments about bringing in Jellaby, but had met with an unexpectedly dark response from his wife. Reginald himself pointedly ignored the entire company. He was perversely even more put off by Julie's propitiation, and complained rancorously about the bitter coffee she handed to him though he drank it all anyway. He then descended into an even more bitter denunciation of Youth and the Pitfalls of Modernity. It was felt to be a relief when he abjured the card table Marty had set up for his pleasure and stalked off to his own chambers, eschewing short-temperedly Marty's offer to ring for his valet.

Almost immediately, the atmosphere seemed to lighten, and Biff turned the wireless on. Maude, in a spontaneous moment of release from Reginald's oppressive presence, agreed to dance with Harris. They were soon joined by Julie and Garth, and Arthur held out his hand to Lucy with the least sardonic bow he could manage. As the young couples were dancing, Marty seemed to gather herself with a little shake and slipped out unseen. When she returned, a new song was just starting up, and she pulled Biff into the dance with the rest of them. Her eyes were peculiarly bright and her color a little high, but she smiled and laughed naturally enough, and soon they were all dancing merrily.

When the clock struck eleven, Maude and Lucy found themselves struggling to hide their yawns. The exertion of the drive and the strain of the day had worn them down. Marty joined them on their way out of the drawing room, muffling a yawn herself. They parted at the stairs, Maude and Lucy taking the ones on the left, closest to the library, while Marty walked a little way toward the staircase on the right which led straight up to the rooms on the other end of the hall from Maude and Lucy.

"Ouch! Oh Luce, help! I've snagged myself on the banister, I think!"

The two young women bent to extricate Maude's dress from an errant nail, trying to free the diaphanous material without causing too much damage. They were still engaged in this finicky task when they heard Julie's heels tap-tapping rather sharply out of the drawing room and toward the doors leading out of the hall and into the conservatory.

"Darling, do wait. It was the merest nothing, you know that!"

"No, I don't know any such thing. Why all the questions about Jellaby, Garth? Why should it matter whether he comes the day after tomorrow or not? What does any of it matter!"

"No, no, of course not, but it is only for you! I should hate to see you cut out of your grandfather's will because of me! There's no need to announce it to the world just yet, is there?

I mean to say, you wouldn't want to upset your grandfather, surely."

Maude and Lucy crouched low, each waggling their eyebrows in a silent language developed during years of boarding school together. They easily agreed they should most definitely not disclose their presence on the stairs while this rather embarrassing—and, needless to say, highly interesting—exchange was taking place.

"Upset Grandpapa! Much he cares! All he cares about is getting his own way. And if I have anything to say to it—and if Arthur has anything to say to it too, I'm sure—he's not going to get his way at all! He can leave all his money to the society for unlettered children for all I care! And the sooner he has the opportunity to do so, the better, as far as I'm concerned!"

"You don't mean that, darling. I love you, but I would hate to think how we would go on if you were to stop receiving what's rightfully yours. And if I'd known..."

The voices disappeared as Garth followed Julie into the conservatory and the doors clapped shut behind them.

"Whew! What was that, Maudie?!"

"Damned if I know, Luce! Trouble in paradise, that's what! I thought they were already engaged, didn't you? Do you suppose they haven't told Reginald yet or something? But it seems almost incredible."

Maude and Lucy made their way up the stairs once again, shaking their heads, unsure what exactly to think about the acrimonious conversation they had just overheard.

"Well, goodnight darling. No rest for the wicked, but perhaps we aren't the wickedest ones around!"

Lucy kissed Maude's cheek. "Goodnight—let's hope tomorrow's a little less thunderous than this evening!" Her words were punctuated by a particularly angry roll of the thunder that had been grumbling and crashing outside all night.

Lucy went into her room and Maude was just about to close her door when she heard a sound on the stairs and paused, wondering who could be coming up these stairs at this time of night. Reginald had shuffled off to bed a long time ago, but perhaps he had rung for his valet? Deciding it was none of her business, Maude started closing her door, only to catch a brief glimpse of a tall figure and wavy brown hair just as her door clicked shut. Biff? Wonder what he's doing up here, she yawned to herself. But as her head hit the soft goose-down pillow, all thought of Biff and Reginald and the rest of the ill-assorted party rushed from her mind. She tossed a few times when especially loud crashes of thunder seemed to almost be in the house itself, wondering in a half-asleep daze whether one of the last few crashes had came from across the hall, but turned over and fell back into a deep slumber, from which she was aroused only by Betsy entering with her early tea.

# BREAKFAST AND A BROUHAHA

Overnight the thunderstorms had turned into a thick, slogging rain and the next morning the windowpanes barely let in any light. Jennings had turned on stained glass lamps in various corners to dispel the gloom. Despite the heavy skies outside, the warm glow they spilled in the breakfast room created a cozy feeling. Entering the breakfast room a little after nine dressed in a yellow frock and grey pullover, Maude compared this warm feeling favorably to the previous night's chill.

The assembled party seemed to be in a much better mood as well. Whether this was due to the fact that Reginald, as was his custom, had not chosen to appear at the breakfast table, Maude refrained from speculating. The gathered company consisted of Biff, placid as ever, if also slightly distracted; Marty, her hair neatly tucked back for a change—it was early yet—and a smile upon her lips; Lucy, already tucking into bacon and kippers; and Harris, plodding through a plate piled high with eggs, toast, bacon, and kedgeree. Garth, looking a trifle haggard, had chosen a chair a little removed from the group, and seemed to have developed an extreme interest in the discussions of parliament and other sundry matters of public interest covered in the local journal of note. Maude, delicately choosing the chair farthest from Harris, wondered if it had anything to do with the heated exchange she and Lucy had overheard the previous night. She almost felt sorry for him, trapped as he was at breakfast with his fiancée's family (was she his fiancée after all?). Even more awkward when the damsel in question had not deigned to appear at all, choosing, instead, to breakfast in bed.

Arthur sauntered in desultorily and helped himself to some eggs and bacon. His crisp light colored summer suit struck a stark contrast to Biff's slouchy brown sweater and indeterminately grey pants and Garth's slightly bohemian, disheveled appearance. "A cheery morn, what? And I gather we are to be further regaled by an additional visitor this weekend."

Garth looked up sharply, Biff gave a worried frown, muttering "It's a bad business, a very bad business" under his breath, and Marty's smile flickered. Her fingers twisted the scarf around her neck and she said more to herself than to anyone else, "Well, yes, I do believe Sir Jellaby is going to arrive either today or tomorrow. Although I wish Father hadn't asked him up. Perhaps he'll be delayed because of all the rain and not be able to arrive at all."

"Would you count yourself so fortunate, Marty?" smirked Arthur. He gave her an understanding smile when she bristled and quite obviously champed her mouth shut against any hasty remarks. Arthur, passing a rather arrogant look around the table, caught Lucy's contemplative and somewhat contemptuous gaze. Her eyes held a little too much amused understanding for comfort. He too fell quiet and tried to sip his coffee nonchalantly. A strained silence settled over the table—Maude could have strangled Arthur for ruining a perfectly nice breakfast. Until his baleful presence, the meal had shown all signs, despite the weather and the previous night's excess of choler, of turning into a fairly pleasant gathering.

For about ten minutes, the silence gave way only to the ring of cutlery scraping against plates and the rustle of newspaper pages. Lucy retreated into her own mind, part of which was occupied with the travails of Pyloria's heroine. Maude shot dirty looks at Arthur and tried to send sympathetic looks toward Marty. Nobody spoke.

Into this silence entered Jennings, uttering a discreet cough and stepping toward Biff.

"My apologies, my lord, but Lord Reginald's valet is a little concerned."

Biff looked up as if he were a startled deer staring down the barrel of a particularly unexpected gun. "Concerned? But what should concern him? Is the fellow alright? Everything alright downstairs, eh?"

"Yes, my lord. It appears that Lord Reginald's door is locked."

"Well—well is that so?" Biff was clearly mystified as to why the valet should expect Reginald's door to be unlocked.

"It is typically unlocked, sir, so that Barstow may enter in the mornings."

"Well—surely he just doesn't want to be disturbed?" Biff was still confused. The lord and master of the household was not known for his pleasant morning demeanor. In fact, he was rather notorious for locking himself into his bedroom when he felt, as he so often did, averse to company—even that of his own valet.

Seeing some of these thoughts flit across Biff's face, Jennings unbent further to explain, "Perhaps I should mention, my lord, Mr. Barstow was particularly instructed by his lordship to help his lordship get dressed in good time so he could go over some papers and prepare for Sir Jellaby's arrival tomorrow. He has knocked a few times on Lord Reginald's door in the past hour, but has met with no response." Here Jennings paused again until he was sure his audience was ready for the next revelation. "Not wishing to disturb you, I have knocked and called out to his lordship myself and received no response." His face remained impassive, but Jennings' shocked tone implied that such obtuse behavior on the part of his employer was an affront he was only overlooking out of a commitment to his duty. Although the knocks of such a lowly personage as Barstow were negligible, it was, in fact, unforgivable of Lord Reginald to have ignored the discreet taps of such an esteemed personage as himself. "Unfortunately it is not within my power to open the door with a key, the only key being the one Lord Timberly possessed. As you may recall, he did not deem it necessary to entrust me with a spare." Lucy, catching Maude's eye at this, had to stifle an unbecoming snort under a spate of coughing. It was evident the wound ran deep in Jennings' honor.

"Do go see what you can do, Biff. I hope Father hasn't fallen or something! Do you suppose he might have slipped in the bath? I do hope—"

"Lord Reginald, my lady, had no opportunity of being in the bath, as his valet was unable to enter his offices this morning," Jennings said awfully, directing a reproachful look at the hapless valet.

"Sir, m'lady, I'm so sorry, m'lady, but I'm afraid his lordship might have had a fall, m'lady, sir," bobbed the nervous little man standing with one foot over the threshold of the breakfast room and one foot waiting in the hall, as though ready to take flight. The poor man was quite obviously distraught and even more nervous to have to explain the matter to such a large audience. "He particularly told me to wake him up, and it's been an hour and there's no response, m'lady, sir. He said particularly that he had to meet his lawyer, m'lady, sir. And the door's locked and there's no response. M'lady, sir."

At this speech Arthur raised a cynical eyebrow, but rose, saying, "Perhaps this does require some action, don't you think, Biff?" and strode out of the room. Without the appearance of haste, he still managed to reach the stairs in short order, followed by a finally galvanized Biff, a flustered Marty, and the ever curious Maude and Lucy (once again waggling expressive eyebrows at each other). Harris followed behind the others, presumably to offer assistance in case his heft and brawn, not to say his medical expertise, were needed. Garth, however, with a great show of reticence, stayed put where he was. Perhaps he felt it imprudent to barge in upon the caustic grandfather of his possibly estranged fiancée.

When Maude and Lucy arrived on the landing outside their rooms, Arthur was thumping loudly on the door and

jiggling the doorknob, calling out "Sir, sir! Uncle Reg!"
Maude's eyebrows disappeared into her curls and she and
Lucy stared at each other, goggle-eyed. 'Uncle Reg!' A sudden
vision of little Arthur, wearing short pants and a torn shirt,
running along beside a younger and more cheerful Reginald
Timberly flashed across Lucy's mind. But 'Uncle Reg' gave no
response even to this term of endearment, and Arthur turned
to Biff urgently. He said without a trace of his usual suave
confidence, "Something must be wrong. Here, help me, will
you?" and turned to shove his shoulder into the door.

Harris's quiet voice stopped Arthur as he tried once again
to push the door open. "Perhaps we should try and force the
lock? Seems like a sturdy door to me."

Arthur turned around to look at Harris, then back at the
heavy oak doors. He acknowledged the value of the doctor's
eminently reasonable statement, but seemed at a loss as to
how to proceed. Although he prided himself on having a
varied career, the exigencies of lock picking had never before
crossed his path.

Biff stood around, still looking struck, and absently
stroking his large, floppy ear. With his other hand he
ineffectively soothed Marty, who was now in the process of
fluttering scarves and beads around in distraction and whose
hair had inevitably come loose.

Lucy, seeing she could be of use, quietly plucked a hairpin
dangling precariously from Marty's head and handed it to
Arthur. His eyes lit up with quick humor at Lucy's presence
of mind in rescuing the errant hairpin and pressing it into
action, but he turned back to the door without a word.

With the combined efforts of Marty's hairpin, Arthur's
delicate ministrations and the doctor's directions, they were
finally able to force the lock and the thick oak doors swung
open with a click. As both Arthur and Harris had been
leaning on the door during their lock picking efforts, this not
unnaturally caused both of them to enter the room with more
haste than elegance, quickly making the acquaintance of the
thick carpet covering every inch of the floor. Without regard

for the unfortunate valet, who was the first thing he could clutch at, Arthur levered himself up, pushing the valet down like a see-saw. The crowd rushed through the little sitting room and into the bedroom, Arthur leading the way.

Maude and Lucy trotted in as well at the end of the pack (they had hung back out of an obligatory sense of modesty, but weren't about to completely bow out). As the motley bunch before them stopped in their tracks, the two were brought to a rather abrupt halt. Lucy saw Arthur check himself at the open door and turn white. His lips clamped shut into a thin line and his hands clenched into fists. Biff, next after him, turned a bright purple instead and covered his face with shaking hands, stepping back to shield Marty. She, however, had bent to retrieve a scarf and, seeing under Biff's extended arm, gave a muffled shriek, holding the errant scarf up to her trembling lips. Harris, who had picked himself up, had shuffled up behind Arthur and stood now looking more bovine than ever, both hands tucked into his trouser pockets. As Biff succeeded in drawing Marty back from the door, Maude and Lucy were finally able to see what had silenced them all.

The room was decorated in the heavy Victorian oak favored in Reginald's youth. A profusion of dark mahogany and elaborate carving lent the room a gothic appearance. Dark velvet curtains still covered the windows. Cracks between the curtains let in a soft diffused light and highlighted the eerie scene before them.

Reginald Timberly lay stiffly convulsed, half out of bed, the tips of his fingers touching the floor, his body arched unnaturally, feet tangled in a mess of sheets and covers, face twisted into a horrible grimace. The lamp at the bedside had fallen off the table, and a mass of broken colored glass lay scattered on the thick carpet along with a few papers.

Maude gasped and stepped forward, not seeming to know what she was doing. Lucy's fingers dug into her arm and stopped her mid-stride. Lucy herself looked a little green around the gills. Sensing Maude's movement behind him,

Arthur glanced around. With a return to a fair approximation of his usual sarcastic smile only belied by a twitch at the corner of his mouth, he said, "Quite right. I wouldn't advance further if I were you." He turned away abruptly and with a faint waver in his voice, snapped out "It's clear enough there's nothing we can do here." He walked a few steps away, and the little group moved with him.

Arthur did not stop Harris from advancing, however, and merely walked a little farther away as if he couldn't bear to see the doctor feel Reginald's unmoving wrist and complete the requisite functions of his profession. Maude and Lucy turned to Biff and Marty, seeking comfort in their friends' company and trying to calm Marty as far as possible.

As the doctor was finishing up, Jennings, having waited decorously by the main door (and keeping the valet there by dint of pure will and a supercilious eyebrow), had made his way over to the bedroom door, unable to keep his curiosity in check. At the sight, his face, more wooden than ever, betrayed nothing. He stepped back, however, and one trembling hand found the doorjamb. After a moment he gave voice to what everyone was thinking. "Is—is he?"

"Yes," Harris replied curtly.

"Oh m'lor'! Oh lor' lumme! M'lor'!" Barstow, no longer held back by the butler's raised eyebrow, had stumbled forward to see what was happening as well.

Jennings stiffened his spine at the sight of his lesser fellow exhibiting such unseemly signs of distress, and thrust the valet out of the door and toward the hallway.

"Better telephone the police." Harris spoke in a grim voice and raised himself from the floor where he had knelt next to Reginald's face and hands. He stepped carefully over the broken glass and came back toward the group standing in the sitting room of the suite.

Arthur shot him a keen look, but said nothing.

"The police! But surely—but why—he couldn't—nobody—but..." Marty trailed off.

"I can't sign a death certificate, Lady Hemming, you can

see that," Harris said gently.

"They'll be much more on the spot than any of us, in any case," Arthur said in a harsh voice and turned away.

"Jennings, perhaps you would be so good as to take the key and have one of the servants stay by the door. The outer door will do." Harris spoke with the authority of his profession.

Jennings gave Harris a slight bow, while Biff, shaking himself out of his stupor, protested feebly. "Do you really think that's necessary, my boy? I'm sure nobody would, would..."

Biff petered out under Arthur's contemptuous, cold gaze. The younger man said tightly, "I'm sure we've all read enough mysteries to have it dinned into our heads that nothing is to be touched." The corner of his mouth still rose with an ironic bent, but all the color had drained out of his face. He retreated from the room with a slow step.

"I do think it advisable, sir," Harris uttered in a low voice, turning a little away from Maude, Lucy and Marty, as though to shield them from his words. Maude instantly marched up to Biff and laid a hand on his arm, outraged at this particularly specious form of chivalry.

"Of—of course, my boy, of course."

Arthur snapped out, "Has that fellow gone yet? What are you standing about for? The police! Now!"

With one final wincing look at Reginald's bedroom door—now shut and locked by the efficient Jennings—Barstow took off down the stairs at a fast clip. Arthur walked out deliberately behind him, followed by the rest of the shaken group.

# A DETECTIVE INSPECTOR AT LARGE

"Rex dear, Brumble says there's a 'phone call for you. I told him I'd give you the message as I was walking in here anyway. Take it in the study, would you? The children will be down from their lunch any minute now, and you know how loud they can get."

Rex Harte raised his head from the local newspaper's highly colored account of a case he had himself put to rest in an extremely unexciting fashion and looked up at the pretty, slim woman who had just entered the room. The two had the same thick, straight eyebrows, although the effect was softened in her face by the addition of two dimples and an adorable snub nose. In his, the brows—now lowering fast—merely emphasized the sharp planes created by high cheekbones and a straight nose. Thick, dark hair and a trick of tilting his head to the side in silent contemplation heightened the impression of a sharp-eyed rook. It was only his mobile mouth and the smiling eyes that saved him from looking like a man carved out of granite.

"Blast! One wretched weekend I take to spend with my sister and they find me even here!"

"I do hope you won't get called away! I can't imagine there'd be anything CID-worthy here in Little Bixby and the only other town for miles around is Timberly—quite as little as this place—and of course Bellingsley, but even that's only close as the crow flies, and much closer to London!"

"Well, nothing for it but to go see what it is I suppose," sighed her brother, unwedging himself from the depths of an overstuffed sofa designed to persistently hold on to anyone sitting in it. He laid down his paper and his pipe (finally smoking nicely, blast it), and made his way out of the cozy, pretty little library and toward his brother-in-law's equally comfortable but stubbornly masculine study.

"Detective Inspector Rex Harte speaking."

"Harte! I'm glad I caught you. Sorry to interrupt the weekend with the family—say hello to Lily, will you—but I've got something right up your alley. Good decor."

"Ha! Good decor! Lily will have something to say the next time she's up in town with Mrs. Holliday, sir! I don't think she'll appreciate having me cut my visit short like this."

"Well, I'll take my medicine when I have to. I must say though, I'm very glad you're on the spot, because the local chaps aren't up to it, and what with it being the lord of the manor and all that, General Potts—he's the Chief Constable there—thought it a deal better if we take over. It seems this Lord Timberly—you can guess where—has gone and gotten himself killed in the middle of a house party, and, from the looks of it, by one of his own family to boot."

"Well if it was in the middle of a dinner party what're the local chaps calling us in for? Nab the fellow with the bloody knife in his hands and wrap it up with a bow!"

"Poison, my dear fellow, poison. And a nasty business at that. There was a doctor on the spot who noticed it right away, and the police surgeon said at first glance it looks like a case of strychnine. He's put the time of death at midnight or before."

Despite himself, Harte's interest was peaked. He did indeed, as his superintendent knew well, like good decor.

"Like that, is it? Well, if you wouldn't mind having Maddock sent down—he isn't the worst of the lot apart from his nasty habit of catching me in my words—I'll head over there right away. Local man at the station my first port of call?"

"Appreciate it, Harte. Yes, Swithon's his name. And you'll find him glad to have you too. I've already got Maddock on the way—I know he's a favorite of yours. Keep me updated.

Hello to Lily and Fred if he's around."

After the superintendent rang off, Rex stood staring at the instrument for a minute, his dark eyebrows furrowing over sharp blue eyes. Setting the instrument down, he gave a brief sigh and went to break the news to his sister and two little rapscallions who would be quite vocally disappointed about Uncle Rex cutting his visit short. They would have to be bribed with promises of ghoulish details about the "Body" and the "Murder Weapon," Rex thought to himself. Perhaps he'd have to throw in a smuggler or two.

*

"And so, sir, I put it to the Chief Constable that it might be best to call in someone a little more experienced," said Inspector Swithon, partly embarrassed to have to call in the CID, yet conscious of a feeling of relief that he was well out of what looked to be an extremely unpleasant and muddled case. His bulbous red nose perspired as he took in the Yard man seated in front of him. He had an air of whimsy that Swithon couldn't but feel was unsuited to a detective, and a trick of tilting his head to one side like a curious bird and smiling in an understanding manner. The fine threads of his suit made Inspector Swithon wonder at the salary the CID was paying these days, and the highly polished shoes, having miraculously survived the muck outside, made the inspector almost envious. Wiping his nose with a large checkered handkerchief, Swithon wondered what this young man with the bright eyes and curious air was thinking.

"Yes, I can see why." Harte nodded over the file in his hands, glancing up from the closely typed sheets to say sympathetically, "Local gentry; not that it should matter, but there it is."

"Exactly, sir." Swithon was relieved to see the sharp blue eyes twinkle. He had thought, when Detective Inspector Harte arrived in a distinctly un-CID-like sporty red convertible, that he might be in for an arrogant young buck.

But Harte, despite his crisply tailored suit and his age (they were making detectives younger and younger these days, thought Inspector Swithon, who had been well past fifty for some time now), had been cheerfully informal and not the least difficult to talk to. "You've got my notes there, and if you'd like to talk it over, I'm happy. I sent my man to pick up your sergeant at the station. He should be here any minute."

"Well, I'd appreciate it if you could give me a rundown of the *dramatis personae* as it were."

"Well, as to that…from what I can tell, it's a mish-mash of people the Hemmings had invited, sir. Lord Bartholomew and Lady Marty Hemming, that is, Lady Hemming being Lord Timberly's daughter. They live with—er, lived—with Lord Timberly. Well—they still live there of course. Seem to have gotten along alright, bar some unpleasantness with Lord Timberly being a little clutch-fisted, but that's common knowledge, and you don't go killing your father or father-in-law over money for roof repairs, do you? Miss Julie, who is Lord Timberly's granddaughter and Lady Hemming's niece, was there with her fiancé, a Mr. Garth Ashford. Seems to be a bit of a fiasco between the two—when I went over there he was looking fit to make a run for it, and she was holed up in her room still, having had a bit of a lover's tiff, I believe. They both live in London. I've got their addresses noted down here. Miss Julie used to live with Lord and Lady Hemming until they moved out here a couple of years ago. Never got on much with her grandfather, although that's no reason to poison the man so far as I can tell. Lord Timberly didn't much like the idea of her marrying Mr. Ashford, however. He's a painter, I do believe. Never heard of him myself, but then that's neither here nor there. Gets fashionable ladies to sit for portraits and that sort of thing. Very much shaken he seemed. And Mr. Arthur Pendleton is Lord Timberly's godson. A gentleman of leisure so far as I can tell. Has a flat in London, comes down here from time to time to visit his godfather. Got a sharp tongue in his head, too. Then again, I don't put any stock in how people react to death. As like as not you'll believe they're the murderer when really they're just mightily upset. Liable to laugh as well as cry, folks are. Why, take Miss Julie—absolutely refused to come out of her room when we first got there, and then wouldn't stop crying, though you wouldn't have thought there was any love lost between her and her grandfather from all accounts! Couldn't get a word of sense out of her until Dr. Witting gave her some powders and packed her off to bed again. And finally there's Miss Lucy and Miss Maude—pair of nicer young ladies you'd be hard put to find. Live up at Bellingsley at Miss Lucy's house."

"Friends of this Miss Julie, are they?"

"No sir, they're young friends of Lord and Lady Hemming. Miss Julie doesn't seem to have much in the way of friends, or at least none as I've ever seen her invite down here. Miss Belling and Miss Grimsworth have visited Lady Hemming on occasion."

"I see. And that's it?"

"That's it, apart from Dr. Harris Witting. He's the local doctor, sir, a good man, Dr. Witting. Lives with his mother, Mrs. Witting, and runs a nice little practice in town. He was on the spot to make sure Lord Timberly was actually dead. Though from what I saw, there could hardly have been any doubt."

"And the body?"

"Taken away by our police surgeon sir, but evident he'd been poisoned. We'll have the photos for you soon. Quite horrific it was, to see his face all crumpled up into a grimace like that, and the body arched fit to be one of those yogis you read about in the papers. Dr. Marston's already sent a message saying it looks like strychnine from his preliminary examination. He'll have results for you later tonight along with a more accurate time of death, but seems pretty clear he was poisoned before he went to bed and died during the night. Everything else's been left untouched and the door locked. The butler locked the door on Dr. Harris's orders before we arrived, so I believe everything is as it was last night."

"Right. Any of the servants involved do you think?"

"It doesn't appear so. The female staff don't really come into it and Lord Hemming's man's sick with this influenza."

"Oh? The butler did it, eh? Or was it the valet?" Harte twinkled at Inspector Swithon.

The inspector chuckled ponderously and said, "Come now, sir. Mr. Jennings has been at Timberly any time these past twenty years, and the valet, Barstow, has stuck it out longer than any other of Lord Reginald's men—going on four years now. In fact, it's their testimony together that might throw some light, sir. Mr. Barstow tried to get into Lord Reginald's apartments—there's a suite—to make ready for the morrow—laying out clothes and whatnot—at half past midnight, and Mr. Jennings had accompanied him upstairs while doing his final rounds before retiring to bed. Both agree that the doors were locked and there was no response to Mr. Barstow's knock. Jennings was in the hall when the valet tried the door. And when he got no response Barstow just accompanied Jennings on his rounds and the two retired to bed. Prior to that, Jennings had been doing his duties with the guests and in the pantry, of course. The footman will vouch for him. And Barstow had been doing his duties downstairs. The kitchen maids and Mrs. Basset—she's the housekeeper—vouch for him. Didn't go anywhere near Lord Timberly since he dressed him for dinner."

"Alright, that lets them out, it would appear, although I'll withhold judgment for now. And I'm going to hazard a guess and say all of these assorted characters had access to some handy strychnine," Harte said politely.

"Well..."

"Tell me all, Swithon, in one fell swoop if you will."

"There is rat poison containing strychnine stored in the conservatory, which anybody who knows it could have walked right into and picked up at any time. The box is half empty too, and the housekeeper who used it yesterday says it was almost full when she took out a little scoop in the late afternoon to spread around the kitchen and larder. But the only persons who say they knew where the rat poison was stored are Lord and Lady Hemming, Miss Maude Grimsworth, Miss Lucy Belling, and the butler, Jennings."

"This Miss Grimsworth and Miss Belling—why should they know where the household stash of poison was kept?"

"It seems there was some discussion at tea, sir."

"Can't say I like these sorts of conversation topics myself, but then, each to his own. Any chance of proving they were the only ones who knew?" With another glance at the inspector, Harte tipped his head to one side, sighed, and said, "All at once, Swithon! I can handle one more fell swoop but that's all, I warn you!"

Pulling another rumbling chuckle from the depths of his belly, Swithon said, "It seems the tea was held out on the porch, sir, at the back of the house—a little terrace it is. And everyone else either was standing a little apart or arrived right then or shortly after, so any one of them could have heard where the rat poison was kept."

"You might as well tell me the worst. Did this fine collection of individuals take it upon themselves to go on some nightly prowls?"

"It appears Lord Timberly retired to his chambers at ten o'clock, Lady Hemming, Miss Belling, and Miss Grimsworth retired at eleven o'clock, and everyone else shortly thereafter. All of them say they went directly to bed."

"Blast. I suppose all of them did prowl around, but it just hasn't come out yet. Alright, until Marston sends in his report with a confirmation of the poison and so forth, that's enough to be getting along with. And now if my sergeant has arrived, I think I'd like to take a look at the scenery and start getting on with it, if you don't mind. You've been more than helpful, and I've no doubt I'll be returning with my tail between my legs in short order."

"Well, sir..." Inspector Swithon gave a friendly grin and held out his hand. "If you CID types can't solve a crime like this, then I've got nothing to be embarrassed about myself!"

# THE ROOK AND THE HAKE

At Timberly, an uneasy silence prevailed. Julie, having treated everyone to a rather amazing display of hysterics—especially for one who typically seemed bored with life itself—had retired to her chamber with one of Dr. Witting's powders, and had remained there, refusing anything other than tea and dry toast. Garth, on the other hand, was very much present with the rest of the company, and seemed inclined to overly offhand speculation after the police's departure. This caused Arthur, who had regained his composure and had treated the police with a good show of arrogance, to raise his cynical eyebrows ever higher, and to became more and more sardonic as the day wore on. Even Marty had almost snapped at Garth's continuous wonderings after she had agreed for the fifth time that it just wasn't possible, and the thing was to find out how it happened. Her hair, which she had dressed at least three times since the morning, spattered bobby pins wherever she went, and the few remaining holdouts met their demise with her constant worrying at the wisps around her face. Harris was quiet, but showed a marked tendency to follow Maude from room to room and to try and engage her in romantically inclined conversation in which she was far from feeling any interest. Rather more distractedly, Marty seemed to be following Biff around, and although she kept darting quick glances at him, responded only briefly to his questions, and didn't inaugurate any conversation herself.

Lucy, finding herself at a loose end, was in no way inclined to participate in the farce that was Maude's dance away from Harris and the doctor's slow yet steady pursuit. If Maude would only give the fellow a direct dismissal once and for all, instead of trying to avoid the topic altogether, she'd be much better off. She wondered a little at this funny reticence but gave up trying to puzzle it out. Maude's kind heart was her downfall, and perhaps even she couldn't be blunt when it came to breaking hearts. Instead of unraveling her friend's romantic problems, Lucy decided she needed to escape the heavy drama suffocating the morning room where everyone else had gathered. Retreating to the library, she sought out a chair that invited no company and settled down with her notebook to plot out Pyloria Braithwaite's next story about her beloved character Holly Galbraith. Perhaps sorting out her heroine's romantic entanglements instead of Maude's would alleviate some of the depression the morning's events had cast over the house party. Soon, however, the Hon. Holly Galbraith seemed to keep getting muddled with Marty, Harris took over her hero, and the villain loomed large in a two-headed combination of Garth and Arthur. Just as the monstrous villain was advancing upon a screaming Holly, Lucy jerked her head up, disoriented. She had fallen asleep in the warm library, ensconced in the large armchair facing the window, with the rain still pattering in front of her.

"I can't help but feel they're going to suspect me, Biff. They must. I gave Father his cocoa, after all! Nobody else saw him after that."

"No, no, my dear, they could never suspect you."

"When did you come up, Biff? I must have fallen asleep right away and didn't hear you."

"Why—why, a while after you, I suppose. I stayed in the library with those young fellows. Just making sure they were being taken care of, you know," Biff stuttered a bit as he said this.

"Biff, Biff, I'm worried. Julie..." Lucy could almost imagine Marty wringing her hands together as she said this, and crouched lower, shamelessly eavesdropping with pricked ears. It would only make Marty and Biff thoroughly uncomfortable if she were to make herself known now, of course. Much better to just lie low.

"Pull yourself together, Marty. For her sake at least. She needs us now."

"No. You're right. We must all stick together, the three of us, mustn't we?"

Lucy was getting a distinctly uneasy feeling in the pit of her stomach. She was sure Maude had mentioned to her this morning that she thought she'd seen Biff come up the stairs, which meant he couldn't have been with Arthur and Harris. Or had he gone back down? Had she said he was holding something? But of course it couldn't be dear, kind, stupid Biff, who shuddered even to think about poisoning mice and rats. At the thought of rats and the conversation the previous day, Lucy frowned. Who had been present? She herself had heard the whole thing although she hadn't participated in the conversation. Could it really only be Biff and Marty (for she didn't count Maude, of course) who knew where the rat poison was kept? For rat poison it was, she was sure about it. The word "strychnine" had already crossed the police surgeon's lips when they had arrived to take the body—Lucy shivered—away. And anyone who wasn't completely oblivious knew there was strychnine in rat poison. And if Marty had taken Reginald's cocoa up to him...Lucy recoiled as an image of Marty's steely-eyed designs for the rats jumped to her mind.

The door clicked behind Marty and Biff and Lucy bent around the back of her chair to stare gravely at the closed door for a moment. She turned back to her notebook once again. This time, however, instead of jotting down the madcap adventures of a flighty heiress, she started making a list of names.

Meanwhile, Maude, thinking it was just like Luce to leave her in her time of need, was getting quickly irritated with Harris. It was only when Harris got perilously close to a marriage proposal for a second time, that her annoyance at his failure to take her hints set off her temper. A kind heart was all well and good, but why should he pester her so when it was quite evident she wasn't interested? She had plunged into a thoroughly uncomfortable interview and had finally succeeded in sending him off with his tail between his legs. She was staring at his retreating form with a mulish frown on her face when the door bell rang. She saw Jennings approach the door and guessed from his especially majestic demeanor that he was preparing to impress the Scotland Yard men the police had mentioned.

In the mood to do battle with whomever crossed her path, Maude started surging ahead with purpose. If these Yard men thought they'd barge in here and start haranguing poor Marty and Biff about Reginald—whom someone should've poisoned a long time ago—they'd have to deal with her. Stepping briskly toward the door, she came to an abrupt stop as Jennings stiffly bowed in two men who did not appear to her to be in the least detective-like. The more smartly dressed one of the two was rather stereotypically tall, dark, and handsome, with piercing blue eyes under thick but shapely dark brows, dressed in a sharply tailored suit. The way he tilted his head and gave a critical look at the butler reminded her of a dark, sharp-eyed, clever bird thinking whether he should pounce on this particular worm or let it go. The other, younger man was almost a ridiculous contrast. He was short, fair and rotund, with the eyes of a bullfrog and the general mien of a hake. It was the well-dressed man's sharp blue eyes that stopped her short, and she found her own frank gaze being returned with interest. Blushing a little, she walked ahead to welcome the two, all plans of battle fading from her head.

Harte offered his hand and was greeted with a smile and a "how do you do" from the damsel with the strong chin and the luminous blue-grey eyes. He turned to introduce Sergeant Maddock, whose eyes were practically falling from his head at the sight of his superior greeting a suspect in such a friendly manner. Sergeant Maddock started rapidly reviewing his conversations with his superior and reflected grimly that there was no Mrs. Harte in the picture. "Yet" he added darkly in his own mind.

"I'm Detective Inspector Rex Harte, and this is Sergeant Homer Maddock. Miss—?"

"Grimsworth. But please, do call me Maude." The words slipped out before they could be helped. But his smile was so genuine, and his eyes twinkled so merrily, Maude decided to ignore her momentary lapse in judgment. "I'm a friend of Marty and Biff's. I think Jennings has gone off in search of them, but won't you come into the morning room? I think we're all gravitating there today."

Following Maude toward the morning room, Harte tilted his head slightly to one side and asked, "That would be Lord Bartholomew and Lady Muriel Hemming?" He received a peal of infectious laughter in response.

"Oh! I'd almost forgotten. Ghastly, isn't it? We never call her anything but Marty. Only old Reginald ever called her that, and even he wasn't usually so horrid!"

Smiling, Harte nodded his appreciation, but said only, "Well, I'll have to just call her Lady Hemming then. A horror, was he?"

"Oh, well, I suppose one shouldn't speak ill and all that, but really nobody could say he was a pleasant person with a straight face, you know. But of course, I'm sure he had his good qualities," Maude offered magnanimously. She then destroyed the blithering blandness of this statement by muttering "Not that anyone ever saw them."

Before he could put any further questions to this enchanting young lady, she had opened the door and ushered them into the morning room.

This apartment bore the mark of an avid Orientalist. The Chinese wallpaper served as a fitting backdrop to the large chinoiserie cabinet on one side of the room, and the many lacquered tables scattered here and there boasted a profusion of porcelain vases, figurines, and japanned boxes. Harte's eyes lit upon a grouping of comfortable chairs upholstered in pale rose. One of these chairs was occupied by a slim young man whose perfectly fitted suit, highly polished shoes, and the gold cigarette case he idly flicked open and close, declared him to be a gentleman of leisure. In the chair next to him sat a stolid, rather blocky but capable looking man. Harte judged him to be the doctor from the neat but sober cut of his suit and the placid air he exuded. Before either of these gentlemen could rise and greet Harte and his sergeant, a wiry young man flung over from where he had been lounging by the window and started forward as though to introduce himself. Half-way across the room he suddenly realized his position in relation to everyone else in the room and hastily receded back into the window embrasure where he had been seated. "Ah, The Painter!" thought Harte to himself.

"Inspector—?" Arthur enquired with a glance of mild amusement toward Garth.

"Detective Inspector Harte. And this is Sergeant Maddock."

"Welcome to our midst, Inspector. We've been eagerly awaiting your arrival. Let me introduce myself. Arthur Pendleton, godson of the deceased," said Arthur with a little grimace, "and this is the esteemed Dr. Witting—our local healer," with a faintly mocking smile. And there, in the window, you see Mr. Garth Ashford—painter extraordinaire and lately—er—" Arthur gave an odd pause, "affianced to the esteemed Miss Julie Bosworth." Harte took quick note of the momentary darkening of Arthur's brow. He was curious to meet the young lady who seemed to have inspired romantic passions within at least two of the gentlemen present. As he was wondering whether the doctor had also fallen for the femme fatale and whether these romantic inclinations had anything to do with her grandfather's demise, the door clicked open.

Standing on the threshold were a feathery, plump woman of about forty-five gazing at him with watery eyes and a tallish middle-aged man with soft, wavy brown hair tinged with grey.

"Lord and Lady Hemming, Detective Inspector Harte," announced Jennings from the doorway.

# QUERIES BEGIN

Harte looked around the large library appreciatively. It was evident that a more austere taste had been softened by the addition of cheerful rugs, comfortable stuffed leather chairs and bowls of flowers cut from the garden. He had asked Lady Hemming where he might set up a home base for interviewing members of the house party and had been led here by a stiff Jennings, who was obviously conflicted about having a stately home such as Timberly invaded by "the police." Through some in-bred butler wisdom, he had detected that Harte's bearing and diction spoke to a family and a background not far removed from that of his employers, which restrained him from looking all the way down his nose at these Scotland Yard men. This led to a quandary: were these men to be treated like gentlemen (as Harte obviously was), or were they to be treated as vermin (as all policemen undoubtedly were)? Refraining from making a decision, he had settled upon a stiff deference. He now bowed them into the library saying in repressive tones, "I hope you will be comfortable here. If you require anything, you have only to ring," and withdrew in a stately manner.

Quite un-awed by this display of superiority and indeed, quite understanding of it, Harte advanced into the room followed by Sergeant Maddock. The sergeant, not understanding the delicate complexities of a butler's mind, was huffily upon his dignity.

"Oh! Hullo!"

Momentarily startled, Harte looked around the room until his eyes settled on a sleek blonde head poking up from a wing backed leather chair reclusively turned away from the rest of the room and toward a window in the corner. Liquid brown eyes met his own with a cool, analytical gaze that made Harte wonder what they made of him.

"Good afternoon. I was led to believe this room was unoccupied and I could have it for my use."

"Why—certainly, I suppose so. You must be the CID men I gather. I'm Lucy Belling."

"Detective Inspector Harte. And this is Sergeant Maddock. I hope we aren't disturbing you."

"No, no. I was getting into a tangle anyway." The sturdy figure rose up and started gathering up her notebook and pen. "I'll leave you to it, shall I?"

"Well, if you wouldn't mind, Miss Belling, perhaps I could just ask you a few questions? As you're here."

Lucy raised an eyebrow and said coolly, "As I'm here. Certainly. What would you like to know?"

Pulling out the chair behind the massive mahogany desk for himself, Harte motioned to a matching chair across from him that faced the window and what little light there was on this stormy afternoon. Turning on an ornate stained glass lamp with dragonflies cresting the shade, he gave an imperceptible nod to Maddock indicating a chair slightly removed and behind Miss Belling's. Witnesses—and suspects—were often more likely to speak candidly if they couldn't see a policeman noting down their every word.

Lucy, however, turned around to grace the sergeant with a frank stare as well. She said kindly, "I suppose you'll be writing down everything I say? Oh don't worry, I don't at all mind. But if you require some more light, do feel free to come closer to the desk, won't you? It's quite a dark afternoon, and I'd hate for you to strain your eyes on my behalf. Or there's a lamp on the little table next to you that might be helpful." She turned around and Maddock stared morosely at the back of her head as he carefully settled himself into the cabriole legged chair. Lucy, having calmly disposed of him, straightened her sensible cotton skirt and matching pullover, seated herself, and said, "Ready when you are."

A quick smile rushed across the inspector's face at this breezy behavior, but his face quickly settled into graver contours.

"Miss Belling. From what I hear from Inspector Swithon, you, Miss Grimsworth and Dr. Witting seem to be the least connected to Lord Timberly. I was hoping I could get from you a slightly clearer picture of yesterday evening."

Lucy contemplated him for a moment and bowed her head. "Of course, Inspector. I can't help but realize one of us must have done it, you know. And if that's the case," Lucy paused, "I suppose the best we can hope for is to get it cleared up as soon as possible, distasteful as this all is. As far as that goes, however, I'm afraid I can't be of too much assistance. Maude, Marty and I went to bed just as the clock struck eleven, and I believe everyone else was still very much up and about. If I'm not mistaken, it must have happened after that time."

"What would be most helpful, I believe, is if you were to start a little earlier in the day—say from about teatime onwards."

"Could he have been poisoned at tea?!" Lucy asked, startled. "I thought—but of course, I don't know—that he could only have been poisoned right before he went to bed?"

"I can't say. It would just help me to get a sense of the setting, as it were."

"Ah! Decor!" Lucy nodded understandingly, thinking about the hours she spent outlining her story settings before actually starting to write. "But of course. Well, let's see. I suppose if you're getting a sense of setting, best to tell you about the main character first. In one word, he was quite unloveable. Oh, always polite to me, of course, but then he couldn't get anything out of me and didn't have a hold over me. For those whom he did though—well, let's just say he could be quite unpleasant. Some stories of how he made his money—not quite above board, as one might say. In short, I should have hated to be his enemy. Marty is his daughter. She's a surprisingly warm, loving woman, given that she's got Reginald for a father. I know I am biased of course, because she's a good friend to me and Maude. But a more loving soul you wouldn't find, even though she *is* scatterbrained, unless you looked to her husband. Biff is a big softy. Rather lacking in the business brains department and always finding himself wrong-footed in whatever businesses he chooses to invest in, but so kind and with such a positive outlook, he never fails to believe it is all for the best. The two never had any children, so they've looked upon Julie as their daughter. She's their niece—Reginald's other daughter's daughter. Her parents are dead, and she has been in the habit of looking upon Marty and Biff as her home. They only moved in with Reginald a couple of years ago, and since then she hasn't been too happy to have to see Reginald whenever she wants to see Marty and Biff. He was rather a turnip when it came to Julie's parents—never helped her mother out after her father died and all manner of things. But she is one of his heirs—" Lucy saw Harte's eyebrow rise infinitesimally, but went on in the same even tone she had been using, "as, I'm sure you know, are Arthur Pendleton and Marty. Engaged to Garth Ashford—an up-and-coming painter who would find it rather easier to up and come if he were married to an heiress, and the granddaughter of a peer at that. At the moment he has the entrée in good houses, but not in the best houses, if you see what I mean. He has a habit of flinging himself around, but I should say he is very much in love with the idea of marrying an heiress. You must have heard, Julie went into a strong fit of hysterics today when she learned of Reginald's death. Seemed a bit overblown, since from all I can tell she was never much enamored of him when he was alive, but there it is. It might have been overcompensating. I don't blame her for putting on a show, really. After all, she must realize it can't look too good for her or for Garth that she and Reginald had quarreled yesterday."

Rather startled with this characterization, but appreciating the incisive commentary, Harte nodded to indicate she should go on.

"Arthur is a bit of a snake—although sometimes a nice one—which is possibly the reason he gets along with Reginald, and in fact, seems to have some real affection for him. I think seeing his body really affected Arthur—although of course he wouldn't thank me for saying it. Quite a ghastly scene, with the smashed glass and papers scattered around and Reginald all tangled up in the sheets. You could see in a glance it hadn't come easy. In fact, the only one who didn't shriek or gasp or something was Harris—Dr. Witting, you know. I suppose one gets used to seeing all kinds of bodies if one is a doctor. A completely unnerving thought."

Lucy paused and, apparently feeling she had given enough of a summation of the characters present, continued calmly. "At tea—we had tea on the terrace. Maude and I had arrived just a short while before. I believe everyone else had arrived a little earlier, around lunchtime, I suppose. The two of us went upstairs and changed, then came down to the terrace. Who was there then? Let me see..." Lucy steepled her long fingers and stared at the desk in concentration. "Me, Maude, Marty—no, Marty came later—Biff, and Harris. Right, so that was all of us. We were chatting, then Marty came in wanting to know where the rat poison was." With a sharp glance at the inspector, Lucy added, "For Mrs. Basset—the housekeeper. I mention this because I know you'll want to know who could have known about the rat poison. It was that, wasn't it?"

In response to her questioning gaze, Harte felt compelled to incline his head and say "I can't confirm anything yet pending the medical examination, but yes, it seems most likely, always assuming there weren't any other handy stashes of poison lying around."

Lucy nodded and continued. "I thought as much. Well, I think Maude and Biff were chatting, and I was nearby, talking with Harris when Marty came in. I know I heard her and Biff talking about the rat poison being kept in the conservatory, so I'm sure—although of course, I don't know—Harris must have too, although from all the effect it had on his conversation, I can't be sure. He plods on and on," Lucy added demurely. "Julie and Garth came on to the terrace right around then. They'd been for a walk by the lake. And Arthur came in just about the same time too, I should think. I don't know whether any of them would have heard about the rat poison, though they certainly could have. Then Reginald came in, and Jennings with the tea. Or—no, Jennings entered first, not that it makes much of a difference, I imagine, but I'd like to be precise. Reginald was grumbling as usual. It wasn't a particularly pleasant tea, all told." Seeing Harte's inquisitive glance, Lucy added, "Just a general feeling of discomfort, you know, because of Reginald's griping. He had that effect on people. I think the party broke up when Julie and Garth went inside—the thunderstorm had started by that time, you know, and I think the lightning was giving Julie a headache. That or the fact that Reginald was being especially blistering. And we all went upstairs to rest and change before dinner. How am I doing so far?"

"Quite comprehensive, Miss Belling. Would you go on?"

"Well, let's see. I think, actually, this might be the part that's most interesting to you. We were to gather for cocktails at eight, but Maude and I came down a little earlier because we saw—" Lucy paused, rubbed her nose delicately as if to prevent a sneeze, and went on. "We saw we were ready already. There wasn't anyone but Marty and Biff around in the drawing room, and we got to talking about the orchid Biff's acquired from some old friend. It's in the conservatory. I..." For the first time, Lucy looked discomposed, playing with the notebook and pen in her hands. "Well, it seems rather horrid to think of it now, but it was all our fault, really. We wanted to see it, but when we tried the door, it was locked. I think Jennings mentioned he had locked it after Mrs. Basset got her rat poison after tea, not thinking we'd be using the conservatory that day. If we hadn't insisted...well." Lucy seemed to give herself a mental shake. "Anyway, we did, and Jennings unlocked the door, and all of us went in to take a look. I should tell you we four were together the whole time—Jennings stayed in the hall so he could welcome people into the drawing room if they came—just admiring the orchid together, you know. Rather marvelous, really. But deadly, as it turned out. Not directly of course."

Harte stopped her before she could get any more involved with the orchid's subtle deadliness. No matter how he appreciated her sharp-eyed characterizations, he had no wish to get caught up in whimsical musings on life and death.

"You're sure the door was locked?"

"Positive. Jennings had to send a footman for the key and everything. We left it unlocked when we came out again and went into the drawing room. I could wish we hadn't, but that won't change anything now. In any case, we went in to cocktails leaving the door unlocked. Julie and Garth joined us in a few minutes, then Reginald. I think Arthur and Harris came in around the same time."

Harte made a note or two on the piece of paper before him and glanced at Maddock to make sure he'd taken down what Miss Belling had said. He hadn't missed the little pause, nor had he been totally convinced that the phlegmatic epitome of composure that sat in front of him had had any real desire to sneeze. He sat quietly and wondered what she had been about to say. What had they seen? Or whom? And how could it possibly matter?

When he looked up from his notes he saw that the young lady seated across from him had gone into a brown study, gazing abstractedly at the notebook in her hands.

"Were you writing? I hope we didn't disturb you. Do you write?"

"Oh!" Lucy looked up, thrown off her stride for the first time, clasping her hands over the notebook as if covering it up would make it invisible. "Oh! No! Nothing, really. Just some reminders for myself, that's all. Anyway, so then we had cocktails, and dinner. You know, I don't really remember anything that would be useful to you. It was a fairly normal dinner party, really. Enlivened by Reginald's commentary about the moral depravity of youth, but I think that was his particular hobbyhorse. After dinner we had coffee in the drawing room once again, and he went up at ten. I remember because he made a point to mention it was ten o'clock—didn't approve of young people staying up at all hours, you know. Anyway, the mood lifted a bit without him. Sounds awful to say that doesn't it? *Nil nisi bonum* and all that. Although why one shouldn't say anything ill of the dead when one could never find a good word for him alive is a mystery to me. We got up a bit of a dance party, and Maude, Marty and I went to bed at eleven or so."

Harte got the feeling Lucy had rather rushed over this description of the evening, but decided to let it go for the moment.

"Did Reginald say anything to anyone in particular? I've heard he wasn't too keen on his granddaughter's choice of young man?"

"Oh! That. Well, I guess there's no use saying he was head over heels about Garth or anything. He wasn't. Can't really blame him, I suppose. Garth's a bit of a—well, he's a bit." Harte nodded understandingly, and Lucy continued a little determinedly, "But there wasn't anything in it, you know."

"I was given to understand Lord Timberly had called his lawyer to summon him especially to change his will to prevent this marriage?"

"There's not much you don't know already, is there?" Lucy queried. "Well, that's true enough. But I think Reginald's changed his will a hundred times if he's changed it once. He would've changed it back, you know. Eventually. Julie knows that. So do Biff and Marty."

Making another note, Harte said nothing, but bowed for her to continue.

"And—and that's rather it, actually."

It was Harte's turn now to contemplate Lucy over steepled fingers. After a minute, during which a faint tinge colored Miss Belling's cheeks, he nodded briskly, saying, "Thank you.

You've been very helpful, you know. I do think you should trust me a little more, but then, you haven't known me long." Rising from the desk, he ushered her toward the library door. "If you have anything further to add, you know where to find me," he said gently, looking into Lucy's troubled eyes. "As you said, the sooner this is all cleared up, the better."

Lucy held his gaze for a long moment and Harte wondered if she would tell him anything more. When he was almost certain she was going to let drop a few gems, she held out her hand, shook his own briskly, and walked out of the library shutting the door softly behind her.

The moment she had gone, Maddock leapt out of his uncomfortable chair, exclaiming, "That's a downy one, sir. Knowing. And not sharing all of it, neither." Sergeant Maddock's eyes grew another size or two to emphasize his point.

"No. But do you know, I get the feeling she might tell us some more yet if I don't push her. I wonder how I can change her mind and get her to trust me?" Harte strode over to the bell by the desk and pulled it.

When the dark scarecrow form appeared at the door he looked up from his notes and gave the butler a smile.

"Could you invite Miss Grimsworth in, Jennings?"

# QUESTION AND ANSWER

Maude entered a bit shyly and paused just inside the door, turning to say thank you to Jennings as he clicked the door shut behind her.

"Please, do come in. Have a seat, won't you? I'm not quite an ogre, I assure you," Harte smiled at her.

"Oh that's not what—" Maude paused, but made a quick recovery, "—what I thought at all."

"Not what Miss Belling gave you to understand?" Harte gave her a quick glance and Maude noticed he had rather sparkling, smiling eyes. The corners of her own mouth turned up in response and she sat down in the chair he had indicated.

"Well, I'll just have to trust you're not quite the bear I've been imagining. Lucy would never call you an ogre. She'd have some other utterly devastating description for you, I'm sure. I don't know anything really, you know, although I do wish I could help. Biff and Marty are great friends of ours, and this is putting quite a strain on the poor dears."

"I'll try to make this as easy as I can then. It's in everyone's interest to get the matter cleared up quickly. Could you just tell me a little about Lord Timberly? Were you well acquainted? Had you had any dealings with him?"

"Pretty well acquainted I suppose. I'd met him a number of times when I visited Marty and Biff or ran into them in town on the rare occasions he went out. He conducted all his estate business from the house, you know. That's not to say I had any personal dealings with him—and thankfully, too! Ghastly fellow." Taking note of Harte's raised eyebrows,

Maude rushed on, "Oh I know, but you really can't quite say he was so sweet and wonderful and will be missed ever so much when it's a wonder nobody brained him years ago, can you? In any case, I'm sure you'd be hard put to it to find one person who truly liked him. Well no, Arthur maybe. Arthur and he seemed to understand each other, and Marty's a good and dutiful daughter of course, but even so!"

"I gather you weren't particularly enamored?"

"Well, I suppose he never did me harm, which I've heard is what he sets out to do to anyone he doesn't like overmuch. Some nasty rumors about how he made his money— apparently he wasn't above a touch of blackmail, though I'd hate to have Marty know I've heard that. But he was quite nasty. Never, of course, to me. I've led a fairly blameless life." Harte had to hide a smile at Maude's evident disappointment at not having anything blackmail-worthy in her past.

"I see. And could you tell me about yesterday? Just take me through the afternoon and dinner, if you would."

"Lucy told you about the conservatory I'm sure. It was locked, and we made Jennings open it to look at the orchid. Biff had been telling me about it earlier in the afternoon, at tea, and I was dying to see it."

"Yes. We'll get to that presently. If you wouldn't mind just telling me a little about tea itself? We can just go on chronologically from there. It'll help me get organized."

Maude started a bit uncertainly, but found her stride as the inspector deftly led her through her story. She repeated almost exactly the course of events Lucy had described, ending with "And that's rather how the party broke up. I got the feeling Biff went after Julie to warn her Reginald was going to change his will, but of course I can't be sure. They both love her like a daughter, you know. Julie's been coming home to them in the holidays since her own mother died. And I believe Marty was quite close with her sister."

"Ah, yes. Miss Bosworth. Is she still very much upset by her grandfather's death?"

"You know, she must be. You wouldn't think it would

you? She's usually so aloof and really, almost bored, with everything. And to see the two of them together yesterday you'd have thought she actively disliked her grandfather—after the high-handed way he was acting, she looked fit to kill him—oh!" Her cheeks turning a fiery red, Maude stopped abruptly. "That's not to say—I mean, well anyone would be upset wouldn't they? He wasn't being anything out of the ordinary, just his usual nastiness. He is her grandfather after all, so I'm sure she's sad he's died and all. She would never. Anyway I haven't seen her since her outburst this morning."

"Outburst?"

"Oh I'm making a muck of things! Well nothing for it but to tell you all, I suppose. She just rather went into a—a tantrum is how I would have described it if she weren't an adult, though perhaps it's better if I call it a nerve storm or something. Look, do you mind if we talk about something else? It rather feels like I'm ratting out my friends' niece, and I'm not sure what for. Disliking your grandfather for being an ass but feeling upset when he's gone and died isn't a crime is it?"

Harte gave a little bow and merely said, "And what about later that evening, when you came down to dinner? About what time was it?"

"Oh about half past seven I should say. Lucy knocked on my door and we went down together."

"Was anyone else around at the time? Any other guests also making their way downstairs?"

A soft blush stole over Maude's cheeks, but her eyes flashed as she said "Only Dr. Witting. He was just coming out of his room when we were at the stairs, but we hurried on without him."

"Oh?" Harte tried to keep the word as flat as he could, but he couldn't help wondering what there was in Dr. Witting's presence on the landing that would cause Maude to blush so, and why the two young ladies had rushed off downstairs instead of more naturally waiting for a moment and walking down with the doctor.

"Well, if you must know, he—he's rather a pain, really. I can't imagine why Marty invited him, unless he invited himself because—because I was going to be here." Tossing her curls, Maude continued, "I know how that must sound, and I don't pretend to be an example of modesty, but I'm not that vain anyway. Goodness knows I'm not one of these fashion plates prancing around. But he's been nosing around for a few months now, and I can't seem to get rid of the dratted fellow." Maude glanced up and directed a beguiling look at Harte. "Couldn't you—couldn't you take him in for something? Just to get him to stop mooning around? Not really pin it on him, of course, but just give him a bit of a scare." She looked away, embarrassed to have been so forthcoming with this stranger who looked at her so kindly, and yet hoping she had made it clear she wasn't interested in Harris.

Giving a little chuckle, Harte responded in a grave voice that almost managed to hide the smile still lurking in his eyes, "If only my hands weren't tied, I'd gladly arrest him on the spot. Unfortunately, 'mooning around' a lovely young lady isn't something I can go around arresting otherwise upstanding doctors for, you know."

Maude's mischievous grin drew another chuckle from Harte. She shrugged her shoulders, saying "Well, it was worth a try—I did hope you'd be more obliging!"

In the background, Sergeant Maddock had stopped to lick his pencil, his eyes sternly fixed upon his notebook. Detective Inspector Harte was a young man, and no wife of course, but really! He'd never seen the inspector talk to a witness like that before! There were limits to everything! Although Maddock had his moments of romantic whimsy, his conservative upbringing in a family of policemen and teachers battled with his softer side, and he continued directing severe looks at his notes.

Perhaps feeling the weight of the censorious gaze burning a hole through the sergeant's notes, Harte returned to his questions.

"So you came down to meet Lord and Lady Hemming."

"Yes. And then, as I said, Lucy must have told you—we went to see the orchid. Jennings unlocked the door and went back into the drawing room to prepare cocktails. We all oohed and aahed over it—really beautiful, actually, and the drollest little thing—and trooped back in to the drawing room. I don't think we even shut the door behind us, never mind locking it. I—I can't quite stop thinking about it."

"I wouldn't worry, you know," Harte said gently. "You weren't to know."

He was gratified by the smile Maude directed at him and said, "Could you tell me a little about cocktails and dinner? Particularly, did you happen to notice if any of your fellow guests handed Lord Timberly his drink, say, or perhaps passed him something?"

"Well of course during dinner the servants did the food—oh but that's not what you mean. I think Garth took him a drink during cocktails, and if I'm not mistaken, got short shrift for his troubles. Reginald sent him off with a flea in his ear—he only drinks—drank—sherry before dinner. He was rather a particular old man. Although quite keen to try some liqueur or other that Arthur had brought with him. I'll say this for Arthur—he did seem to have a genuine affection for Reginald, even though he can be quite trying."

Harte directed a quick glance at Maddock, who was scribbling furiously, but said nothing as Maude continued blithely.

"And at dinner—no, I can't think anyone—any of us, I mean, gave Reginald anything. There was the little thing with the wine, of course, but that's not really what you mean. Biff just knocked his—Reginald's—glass over. But that's not giving him anything is it?"

"Did the butler replace the drink?"

"Oh yes of course, Jennings is always on hand—oh!" Maude stopped, and gave Harte a confused look. "But—well, oh, yes."

"Yes?"

"It's nothing. Oh don't think too much of it will you? It's just so silly. Biff just passed his own glass to Reginald because of course nobody had had a chance to even sip any wine, we had all just sat down. And really he couldn't have—even if he ever would, and Biff is the kindest most soft-hearted soul you could ever meet—but he really couldn't have slipped anything into the glass he handed Reginald without all of us noticing. It rather drew everyone's attention, you know. Oh don't be too ghastly and think Biff had anything to do with it!"

Maude was sitting on the edge of her seat now. Seeing her troubled face and fists clenched in her lap, Harte made haste to assure her that of course he would think nothing of so minor an incident—negligible really—and decided to move on to coffee.

"Well at coffee—who gave Reginald his cup? Marty was pouring, of course. Sometimes she can do the grand dame bit quite well, you know. But she was just pouring each and holding it out for the next person. I think Julie—or no, was it Garth or Harris? Well one of them. I think they were all around the same spot. One of them gave Reginald his coffee. I wasn't looking really. And after coffee Reginald went upstairs, of course."

"Did anyone go up to see him after he went upstairs?"

"Oh no—no, I don't think so, really."

Harte gave Maude a quizzical look. "Miss Grimsworth—"

"Maude, please."

"Maude—thank you. I know this is difficult for you. These are all your friends, people you care for. But don't you see? If I don't have the entire picture, I can't find out the truth. And if I can't find out the truth, none of your friends will be cleared of suspicion. Your innocent friends would have to live with the guilt hanging over them forever."

"But surely you can't suspect...?"

"I have to suspect everyone who had a motive. And I can tell you—you, Miss Belling and Dr. Witting seem to be in the clear, but everyone else—"

Maddock's eyebrows were rising high enough to risk

disappearing from his face altogether to hear Detective Inspector Harte being so indiscreet. Perhaps it was just a technique to get the witness to spill some details? Miss Grimsworth had obviously forgotten that the sergeant was in the room, but the inspector had to be aware, surely?

"Well. Well it really has no bearing on anything."

"Even so," said Harte gently, "if you would trust me?"

Looking up into the keen blue eyes, Maude blushed rosily again, as a sudden shyness overcame her. As her own wide blue-grey eyes met his, she seemed to make a decision and sat a little straighter.

"Well—alright, I will. Marty went up to give Reginald his glass of milk or cocoa or whatever it is. She does it every night, you see, so it can't possibly have any bearing on it. Besides, the kitchen prepares it of course. But there it is. We all danced a bit and Marty came and joined us when she got back downstairs. After about an hour or so Lucy, Marty, and I went upstairs. Marty went up the other stairs. Lucy and I took the ones on the left, you see. We're the only ones on that side of the house with Reginald. Marty took the stairs to the right, which are closer to her room on the other end of the landing. And..." Maude paused, caught Harte's eye, and continued with a rush, "well I've decided to trust you and I'm going to. I just hope you won't go around arresting any of my friends. Although from your reluctance to arrest Harris, even if I do think he deserves it for being a pest of the first order, even if he *is* a good doctor, I suppose you might not clap handcuffs onto the first person you see."

Tilting his head to accept this glowing, if slightly entangled, encomium, Harte waited for what Maude would say next. Maddock, meanwhile, relaxed his shoulders slightly. Perhaps the inspector's unorthodox methods were getting somewhere after all.

"We were on the stairs and my dress snagged on something and Lucy and I bent down to get it free. That's when we heard Julie and Garth come out, and it seemed as though they were having a bit of an argument. Not quarreling exactly, but—but—a lover's tiff or something."

"Oh?" Again trying to keep the expression out of his voice, Harte wondered what was to come next.

"And they went into the conservatory. I'm sure it's a wonderful place to have a quarrel, you know," Maude's voice took on a musing note. "In fact, with all that greenery and room to rail about it, practically the best spot to have a quarrel!" Noticing Harte's amused gaze, she went back to her story. "That's really about all I know. We went up, not wanting to eavesdrop or anything. Not that we could, really!"

Harte gave her an appreciative glance, understanding quite clearly that both Miss Belling and Miss Grimsworth had been dying of curiosity, and if there had been anything to be heard, they would have found a way to remain on the stairs a bit longer.

"Thank you, Miss—Maude. You've really been very helpful. Would it be alright if I asked you back in for some questions later if I need to?"

"Yes of course—Rex?" Maude's strong features were transformed as she smiled, gazing up at the inspector. He gave a smiling nod in response, making Maddock's ears wiggle dangerously and his face take on an even more fish-like appearance than usual.

Rising from her seat, Maude looked at Harte directly and was silent for a moment. "I—I did see someone else come up the stairs Lucy and I took to go upstairs. It looked like Biff. I can't be sure. I wish I hadn't told you, but there it is. I shall feel guilty forever until you find the real killer, so do be quick about it won't you?"

Taking her outstretched hand, Harte gave a short bow. "I will. As I said, you can trust me." And on this excellent note of understanding, Maude departed, leaving him staring at the closed door for a few minutes.

When he finally turned around, Maddock was pleased to see him back to his usual brisk and business-like self.

"We'll want to go into who did give Lord Timberly his cocktail—whether Mr. Ashford did in fact do it, or whether he just received his usual sherry from the butler. And the coffee too. And the wine."

"Ah, I was wondering if you'd noticed that, sir."

"I always notice everything, Maddock! You'd do well to remember it instead of staring at me fit to scare a goose out of laying eggs!"

"Ay, sir, that's how it is, is it?"

"No more of your guff, my lad. I'll do very well when I've spoken to a few more witnesses."

"I don't think they'd all be as charming as the last one, sir, if you'll excuse me," Maddock said with an inexpressive face.

"Damn you! None of your insolence! Let's get that blasted doctor in here and see if he can add anything to it. And may as well get the painter fellow lined up too."

# THE DOCTOR AND THE PAINTER

Dr. Harris Witting entered with the measured tread of a man who knows his own worth and is confident in his chosen profession. Detective Inspector Harte had to suppress a momentary annoyance with this stoic fellow who had been expressing amorous (and thankfully, the thought quickly passed through his mind, unrequited) intentions toward Miss Grimsworth. Firmly tamping down this line of thought, Harte indicated the chair he wanted Dr. Witting to take. When the doctor was seated, the inspector started by asking him to describe the other guests and the previous day's events.

"I really don't know what I can tell you to help you," Witting said ponderously. His manner made him appear quite middle-aged, although he seemed to be close to Harte's age and couldn't have been much above thirty-two. Harte found it impossible to imagine why this pompous fellow thought he would make a good match for Miss Maude Grimsworth's delightful, sparkling personality.

"Lord and Lady Hemming are very kind hosts. Lord Timberly I knew a little—I am his tenant. I took over the practice from the previous doctor, who retired a few years ago. Lord Timberly and I would meet occasionally, but I never had cause for any trouble with him, though he could be a little short. His godson I don't really know. Miss Belling and Miss Grimsworth are friends of mine." This brought a grim twitch to the corner of Harte's mouth, but he remained quiet as the doctor continued. "And Miss Bosworth and Mr. Ashford I met for the first time. Yesterday I arrived a little before tea. I had an appointment to see Lord Timberly about some matters regarding the practice—nothing too important, really, just extending the lease and improvements and so forth. He was in a bit of a crusty mood. I met with him briefly just after lunch, when I arrived. Afterwards, I went up to my room for a little while, and came down for tea. Tea was a little strained. It seems Lord Timberly was not too happy with his granddaughter's fiancé, and I believe he seemed a little upset at Lord Hemming as well. Lord Hemming isn't quite as hawkish as his father-in-law when it comes to matters of business."

"Were you nearby when Lady Hemming came in?"

"Do you mean was I there when they were discussing the rat poison? Nobody can talk about anything else, you know," Witting said apologetically. "I must have been on the terrace of course, because I was there when Lady Hemming arrived, but I can't say I remember any mention of rat poison. Of course," Witting bowed, "you have only my word for it. As far as I can tell it was around the time other people were entering the terrace. There was some tension between Julie—Miss Bosworth—and Lord Timberly, and some talk of changing his will. Of course Miss Bosworth and Mr. Ashford did not appear overly pleased about that, and I believe Arthur Pendleton wasn't too happy either, but of course I can't say. Then we all broke up, and went upstairs to change for dinner."

Harte tilted his head to one side and silently noted that Dr. Witting had, despite his staid and innocuous manner, managed to insinuate motives for a number of people. He bowed to indicate the doctor should continue his narrative.

"When I went down for cocktails—I believe I was the last one there—again, the atmosphere was a little strained. I believe Mr. Ashford gave Lord Timberly a cocktail, but I'm afraid not too many of us made an effort to speak with him. I did go up to him—I felt it only my duty, because although Lady Hemming invited me, I was really a guest of Lord Timberly's. I believe we just chatted about this or that. I can't quite remember. I know he mentioned his lawyer was arriving the next day. From something I overheard him tell Arthur, I think it was to change his will. And then at dinner, of course, the mood was still quite tense. It didn't help matters that Lord Hemming spilled Lord Timberly's drink and had to give his father-in-law his own glass of wine. And then of course at coffee, I'm afraid, it was quite unpleasant. Overall not really a relaxed party, even though Miss Bosworth did try to reconcile with her grandfather, took him his coffee and everything."

Harte found his dislike for the young doctor growing, but said evenly, "And after dinner, sir?"

"After dinner I chatted with Arthur for a little while in the library before we both went up. He had promised to go see his godfather before turning in for the night, and Lord Timberly didn't like staying up late after he had withdrawn for the night. He must have gone up at about a quarter past eleven. He came down again—it can't have been more than fifteen or maybe twenty minutes later. We stayed chatting until midnight, when he went out for about half an hour— right around the time we had seen Garth crossing the hall towards the steps at the left. I wondered if he might have had some idea of talking to the chap. Arthur returned at half past twelve—I remember because the clock struck the half hour— and we stayed in the library for another half hour or so, when we both retired to our separate bedrooms. I hope I have been helpful?"

Understanding this as the doctor's conclusion, Harte rose, forcing himself to shake the man's hand and lead him to the door. "Very helpful, thank you. A most detailed précis, as I should expect from a doctor. I may need to ask you some more questions later, but for now this will give us something to go on."

"Thank you," Harris bowed. "I do hope I haven't misled you in any way. I have no desire to cast aspersions or suspicion on anybody, but realized it was my duty to tell you the unvarnished truth." And on these magnificent words, Dr. Harris Witting left the library.

"Well! Talk about casting aspersions!" Harte exchanged

glances with Maddock.

"I wouldn't have thought it of him. There's venom there, sir, you mark my words. Seems like a nice chap to begin with, and slides in all those little daggers here and there!"

"No, Maddock, not a nice chap at all. I begin to see why Miss Grimsworth should dislike him so. Unfortunately, being unlikeable doesn't make one a murderer, and he has no motive and no opportunity so far as I can see."

"Ay sir, but poison's a doctor's trick, mind! Nothing easier than for a medical man to get his hands on a deadly substance and know how to use it too."

"All the more reason he would avoid it! Next you'll remind me of the Borgia woman and tell me poison's a woman's weapon and I should arrest Miss Grimsworth or Miss Belling. No more of your jumping to conclusions, now, and we'll see what the painter has to say for himself, what do you say?"

\*

Mr. Garth Ashford came in, looking rather the worse for wear. Having discarded his previous bluff attitude, he now seemed febrile more than anything else. His tie dangled askew and his cuffs were decidedly limp. Maddock immediately assigned him an as-yet-unknown secret in his mind, and laboriously took notes as the painter flung about the room, refusing to take the seat Harte had proffered, choosing instead to pick up a cigarette from the carved wooden box on the table and twiddle it unlit between his nervous fingers.

"I don't know what you can want with me. I don't even know these people, really. I have no idea who could have committed this dastardly act. All I want is to take Julie away from here—it's bad for her, you know, the atmosphere! And what with her grandfather being beastly to her—although that's neither here nor there because he was beastly to everyone! But of course neither of us could have done it. We didn't even know where the poison—if that's really what he died of—was kept! We weren't there at all!'"

"Weren't where, Mr. Ashford?" Harte asked quietly.

"Well on the terrace of course! Everyone gossiping about rat poison. It's unnatural, I tell you!"

"So you didn't hear the conversation?"

"We weren't there, I tell you! We'd gone for a walk by the lake, don't you know. Just got back from it in fact, didn't hear a word! And besides, I never went into the conservatory so I couldn't possibly have gotten it!"

Seeing Maddock had noted down that Garth Ashford seemed to know exactly when the conversation about rat poison had taken place and where the poison was kept despite having been nowhere near the terrace, as he claimed, Harte decided to move on. In the back of his mind he heard Maude's voice talking about how Julie and Garth had gone into the conservatory to "have it out" as she had put it.

"Sir, if you could please begin with your friendship with Miss Bosworth, and then tell us about yesterday?"

"We're engaged, dammit. I love her! That grandfather of hers kept trying to tell her I was just after her for the money but of course I wasn't—I'm not. And I've proven it to her. I don't know why she doesn't believe me. Must've been the Pendleton fellow. I know there used to be something between them, but I don't care a whit about that. It's all over and done with anyway. Rather snake-like I think him. Always whispering things here and there. And won't say a word about the fact that he went to have a drink with the old man last night, I'm sure! But he did, you know. Most definitely he did. Some deadly foreign liqueur too! I'd investigate him more if I were you instead of wasting your time on questioning people who have nothing to do with it!"

"Yes. I'll be talking to him next. Could you tell me about yesterday evening? When did you come down for cocktails?"

"Julie and I came down together. They've posted me up in the rafters, but we'd said we'd meet on the landing and go down together to show the old fellow what's what. And we did too, dammit, but we ran into that Pendleton fellow by the stairs and he came in with us. I think Witting was present as well. We'd all gathered by then."

"Did you take Lord Timberly a drink during cocktails?"

"Who's been telling tales? Trying to pin it on the outsider! I won't have it! No. Of course I was trying to do the friendly, but the old man would have none of it. Almost became quite rude too. Not," Ashford added hastily, apparently thinking rudeness might create a motive for him, "that he was excessively rude or anything—just crotchety, you know. Gout. Anyway," he rushed on, "the old fellow was busy needling everyone else. I heard him grouse about something with Witting. Some old lady he knew or something. Garfield. Although then they started talking about hats, so who knows, maybe the poor old fellow's mind was wandering—I mean, the man seemed to see me as a damned fortune hunter—and Witting was attending him or something. Dinner was quite, quite strained. I'm a painter, you know, I feel these things. And after dinner, when Julie tried to make friends, he wasn't ready to hear a word. Quite upset her, poor thing, very fond of her grandfather, you know." Blithely contradicting himself, he went on, "In any case, Julie and I went upstairs soon after the dancing broke up. Didn't want to hang around with that snake Pendleton and Witting. Although the doctor's alright, really, but such stolid company is nothing for the painter's mind! Nothing!"

"Did you and Miss Bosworth have a disagreement?"

The fretful fingers pinched the cigarette, crushing it in half. Ashford looked warily at the inspector and paused before he answered. "Of course not, of course not. Just a little lover's tiff, you know. Nothing major. Blown over already! But we both went to our beds right away, so there wasn't much chance of us quarreling or anything like that, you know. Just went straight upstairs. Into that dammed draughty room where they've put me," he added querulously.

"I see." Standing up, Harte said, "That will be all for now, Mr. Ashford. Thank you for your help. Would you be so kind as to send Miss Bosworth in?"

"Here I say—I should be here when you question her, don't you think?"

"You're welcome to stay, of course, if she so desires. Or if she would like, she could have Lady Hemming here to support her." Harte nodded coolly to Ashford who stayed looking at him disconcertedly for a moment and finally turned and hesitantly zig-zagged away from the library.

"That one's scared sir."

"Thank you, Maddock, I have eyes in my head. I wonder what the story really is with him and Miss Bosworth. And he's got his knife into Arthur Pendleton too."

"If you'll excuse me, sir, there's quite a few who've expressed dislike for Mr. Pendleton."

"Not Miss Grimsworth. She seemed to at least say he actually got on with Reginald Timberly."

Maddock decided it was prudent to ignore this lapse on his superior's part in favoring one witness over the other for no good reason as far as he could tell, unless large eyes and a charming smile could be called a good reason. Blinking disapprovingly he went toward the door to respond to the light tap that had sounded on it and let in Jennings, carrying a welcome tray of tea.

*

Garth returned to a room filled with strained silence. Everyone was making a pretense of nibbling at sandwiches and sipping tea, but really trying to studiously avoid any eye contact. Marty wore a strained look and was trying to make small talk with an unhelpful Arthur; Biff looked as though he could use a stiff drink and mumbled responses here and there to Harris Witting; and Julie had again refrained from making an appearance. Garth moved indeterminately toward Lucy and Maude, perhaps feeling they would provide the most sympathetic ears. He was mistaken in Maude, who had already written him off as a wastrel and had sidled off to Marty's side as soon as Garth seemed to be making his way toward them. Lucy shot her a wry look but understood that bearing the brunt of Garth's confidences was her penance for having left Maude alone to fend off Harris Witting's romantic declarations the previous day.

"I hope it wasn't too rough?" asked Lucy solicitously and not a little curiously. Garth was inspiring a new character in the back of her mind and she thought this would be a good opportunity to study him up close. Sure enough, he launched immediately into a vivid description of the encounter and tried to make her believe he had had Inspector Harte eating out of his hand in less than a minute. Having met the cool-headed Harte, Lucy had some difficulty believing this, but she savored the conversation as a character study and nodded her head to go along with Garth's descriptions.

"And I mean, the nerve of the fellow to suggest just because I hadn't received a warm welcome from the old man I should want to do away with him! I mean to say, I told him directly it was no such thing and he'd been a terror to everyone—positively a doddering fool! I'm convinced he was almost senile. Why, I heard him discuss some Mrs. Garfield with Witting quite normally—sharply even—and the next thing you know he's talking about hats! Ridiculous! Mad as a hatter, I say! Possible he even took the poison himself!"

Lucy tried to hedge him off gently, quite embarrassed for him. He was making utterly fatuous statements in a none-too-quiet voice, and she hoped Biff and Marty couldn't hear him at the other side of the room. She murmured soothingly and tried to turn the topic. In this endeavor she was almost undone when she met Arthur's eye and turned away from his smirk only to catch Harris looking up at her sympathetically. Surprisingly, it was Arthur who came to her rescue, strolling over and saying lazily, "Must you monopolize all the beautiful ladies, Ashford? Lucy, would you care to come see the little knick-knacks there? Uncle Reg had a really marvelous collection of Louis IV snuffboxes, you know." She followed him with relief to a glass-topped table and lifted the lid to admire the delicate little items.

"I would thank you, but I'm afraid you'd go back to being odious," murmured Lucy *sotto voce*.

"Never underestimate me, my dear, I have a soft spot for writers," responded Arthur not unkindly.

Lucy flashed a quick glance to see if he was being malicious but found him looking genuinely amused, not a trace of his usual smirk on his face. She suddenly discovered a deep interest in a gold snuff box inlaid with mother of pearl. Pyloria's accomplishments weren't something Lucy liked to make public. She had been at a few too many dinner tables where her host had laughed at the maliciously witty depiction of one of her characters, failing to realize the author was sitting at his table and had, in fact, found her inspiration for the ridiculous character in her host himself. So far as she knew, only Maude knew who Miss Braithwaite actually was. How had Arthur found it out?

As if reading her mind, he said smoothly, "I'm afraid you're a little too good at your caricatures, my dear. If I'm not mistaken, in your last epistolary example, James Sutton rather resembled our dear Biff, didn't he? And I know a certain lady who would be appalled if she laid eyes on your Lady Barnabus character. When I want to find out something about someone I'm interested in, I do have my ways. Your keen eye just made it a little easier."

Amazed, now, that he seemed to have actually read her stories (and also a little flattered), Lucy looked up once more, a glint of curiosity in her liquid brown eyes.

"My dear, I believe I should call myself a fan, if that's the term they use." And with a little bow Arthur removed the snuffbox from her hands, slipped it back into place, and gently closed the glass top. He moved toward Marty to get a refill of his teacup, leaving Lucy to stare after him.

"Wonders will never cease," she mused, feeling quite at charity with him, although appreciating that if one were to get on his wrong side, Arthur might make a formidable enemy. She silently wished him good luck as Jennings entered to escort Arthur to the library for questioning.

# THE GENTLEMAN OF LEISURE

Harte looked up from the envelope of papers a young constable had delivered not five minutes earlier and nodded at Sergeant Maddock.

"Report's in—it was strychnine alright, and most likely from the rat poison. Swithon's attached a note to say the amount of poison in the tin doesn't tally up with what Mrs. Basset told one of his sergeants, and there was a little spilled about the tin, as though someone had got it in a hurry. The housekeeper said she was very careful with it when she took out however much she needed. Seems like we're right about the rat poison being the murder weapon. Now all we've got to do is to find who snuck it out, fed it to Lord Timberly, and there, it's all wrapped up!"

Maddock shook his head at his superior's lighthearted comment and walked over to open the door, where a light tap had sounded.

Arthur Pendleton entered in a smart grey pinstriped suit with his hair set precisely and the usual faintly amused smile hovering on his lips. Walking slowly to the desk, he pulled up his sharply pressed trousers with great precision and sat down, crossing one leg over the other. Still smiling, he bowed his head toward Harte.

"Good evening, sir. Kind of you to come."

"Oh not at all, Inspector. It didn't suit me to be dragged in screaming."

"I shouldn't say we would stoop to that just yet. If you wouldn't mind giving me your observations of yesterday?"

"Reginald was out to be a horror to everyone. We had an

unpleasant tea, followed by a brief respite, an even more unpleasant cocktail hour and a thoroughly unpleasant dinner. We went to bed and woke up to find Reginald had been murdered by one of our number. I'm sure the murderer was not alone in breathing a sigh of relief. I was not amongst them."

"Remarkably brief and precise. If you would tell me a little more about tea, sir—did you hear the conversation about the rat poison?"

"I make it a point never to eavesdrop on the boring domestic matters of the houses I visit."

"Just so. But were you aware of the location of the rat poison?"

"Still not having a clue where it may be, I can't say I was or that I am."

Getting rather irritated with the self-satisfied smirk, Harte tried a different tack. "Did your godfather say anything about any quarrels or arguments he had had with any of the guests when you met him for a *digestif* after dinner?" Glad to see the question had finally succeeded in at least making the smirk waver, if not completely disappear, Harte waited patiently.

"No, Inspector. And I need hardly wonder who gave you that tidbit of information. The ever talented Mr. Ashford, no doubt, found it fit to share with you that I intended to have a glass of Fernet Branca—a particularly bitter liqueur which would nicely mask any dollop of rat poison I should add to it—with my godfather, who had intended to cut me out of his will for no fault of my own. Or perhaps it was darling Marty, who found it inconceivable that her beautiful niece and her soft-hearted fool of a husband should suffer for their stupidity—the one in choosing a life partner, the other in his business affairs—and that she should herself lose her inheritance because of it. Perhaps you wouldn't believe me, but I had a fond regard for old Reginald. Greater than any of his blood relatives, and certainly more than any of the guests assembled here. We did share a glass of Fernet, during which time I tried to convince him it was a foolhardy business to try and force Julie to marry me by threatening her with being cut out. We've had this conversation before, and it went much the same as it usually does. It was an unfortunate notion then and it remains so today. He did not agree, but I could see it would only take a little more cajoling until he at least left me out of this ill-conceived notion. He could cut us all out with my good wishes so long as he didn't tie it up in this absurd way—leave everything to the society for unmanicured lawns, so far as I'm concerned. And so he might have if he had lived to see another day—and his lawyer. But you're barking up the wrong tree here. My godfather was not in a particularly good mood, and, now I think of it, might already have been suffering from the ill effects of poison. He expressed the hope that the Fernet would settle his stomach. But when I left him he was alive and kicking and, although you may be loathe to believe me, had not ingested any poison on my behalf."

"We shall certainly make note of your statement, sir." Harte's sharp blue eyes surveyed this prickly customer coolly. "At what time was it that you left him?"

"I went to see him a few minutes past eleven. Say ten minutes, or even a quarter past. I had been sitting in the library with that pompous ass Harris. As I walked to the stairs I heard Julie and Garth going at it—or Julie going at it and Garth trying most unconvincingly to prove he hadn't married her for her money, but for love. I returned at half past eleven and stayed chatting with Harris until about one o'clock, at which time we both went upstairs."

Harte's face was wooden as he asked, "Did you hear any of what Miss Bosworth and Mr. Ashford were arguing about?"

"No, and I had no intention of lurking around. Lovers' tiffs are as boring to me as domestic matters. I do not make a habit of listening in on them."

"And where were you about midnight, sir? Did you, perhaps, have a conversation with Mr. Ashford?"

"Midni— I went to the cloakroom. I shouldn't refine too

much upon the doctor's precision of timing, if you would, Inspector—for that's where I gather you've received this piece of misinformation. He was two sheets to the wind by the time I went to the cloakroom for a few minutes, and hardly discernible when I helped him up the stairs later. We did see Mr. Ashford go upstairs, but I had no wish to speak with him."

"Thank you, sir. Did you happen to notice when Miss Bosworth went upstairs?"

"No, damn you."

"I'd like to go back a little way if you are amenable. You said you didn't care if Reginald cut you out of his will. If I may, sir, what is your financial position?"

"None of your damn business." Arthur, no longer the cool pinstriped figure that had entered the room, was quickly losing his temper.

"I'm afraid I have to ask you—and find out—as I must for all the heirs, what the financial situation is. It has a bearing upon the case, and," Harte added apologetically but with a glint in his eye, "I'm afraid I shouldn't recommend obstructing the course of justice in this manner."

"It's like that, is it? Well, you can take it from me I am in no need of Reginald's millions."

"What is your source of income, sir?"

"None of your business."

"And how do you spend your time, sir? Do you have any business concerns or investments?"

"I'm a gentleman of leisure with private means, my good fellow. And that's about as much as you'll get out of me. I would recommend looking more closely at that bounder Ashford if I were you, instead of wasting time in following red herrings."

Harte merely bowed and allowed Arthur to exit the room. Turning slowly to Maddock, he nodded.

"Just a few points, sir. This time discrepancy with the doctor's account."

"Yes, that will require going into. I shouldn't say myself

the doctor appeared to be a drinking man. And could you just read back your notes on what he said about Mr. Ashford? You know what I mean."

Maddock shuffled through his shorthand notes and read back to Detective Inspector Harte, "As I walked to the stairs I heard Julie and Garth going at it—or Julie going at it and Garth trying most unconvincingly to prove he hadn't married her for her money, but for love."

"Yes. Have I commended you on your shorthand skills recently, Maddock? Invaluable, you know, invaluable. It appears Mr. Ashford and—Mrs. Ashford?—may have been keeping a little secret. And if that's the case—well, let's just say it looks rather black for either or both of them."

"I'd say it's him, sir. I'm not one to judge hastily, but no gently bred girl like Miss Bosworth would poison her own grandfather!"

"You are exactly the one to judge hastily, and we have no idea whether Miss Bosworth has been gently bred or not! Come come, Maddock, just a little while ago you were convincing me one of these young ladies is a Lucrezia Borgia! Keep an open mind, Maddock! How often do I have to tell you it's no use jumping to conclusions? Sometimes I wonder why I keep you around, unless it's to fill up my head with all sorts of preconceived—and ill-conceived—notions!"

"Possibly my wonderful shorthand skills, sir," Maddock said softly, his large eyes twinkling in response to his superior's denunciation.

"Damn you! You'll go back on the beat yet, my good fellow! But if you do like jumping to conclusions, tell me this: I wonder how or why Mr. Pendleton knows about this supposed marriage?"

"I did notice, sir, there seems to be a bit of—er—history, as you might say—with Mr. Pendleton and Miss Bosworth, sir. I wouldn't be surprised if there's more than what we've heard so far about them."

"Yes, I wonder what the story is there? It seems quite evident there's something, but I can't quite tell why whatever it was should have turned into—how did he phrase it—an 'unfortunate notion.' He seems to have kept an eye on Miss Bosworth's doings, and I think I'd like to keep my eye on this cool customer. And I wonder what the lady's thoughts are on the matter? I think we'll let the fair damsel stew a little more, shall we? It seems as though she had a bright and clear motive to do away with her old grandpater, and it'll do well to go more into Mr. Ashford's movements last night as well. Get Lord Hemming, would you? And while you're at it, put in a call to the Yard and see if they can find out the marital situation of Miss Julie Bosworth—or Mrs. Garth Ashford as she may very well be. I won't say I quite believe Mr. Pendleton either. A bit too quick to admit he had that drink and just how easily he could have poisoned his godfather, don't you think?"

"That's a mighty cool one there, sir, like you said. He'd slip the rest of 'em some poison and say calm as can be that he had the means, motive and opportunity, and he'd still go free!"

"Hm. There you go jumping to conclusions again. Free yourself of the habit, Maddock. Although I can't quite see him doing this particular deed."

"Would that be because Miss Grimsworth said he had a regard for his godfather, sir?" It wasn't possible for Sergeant Maddock's large, fish-like face to wear a sly expression, but the beguiling look in his eyes and the grin on his face had the effect of making Harte swear once again and threaten to throw his subordinate back on the beat. Thinking it prudent, Maddock suggested that he should go search out Lord Hemming and retired in short order.

\*

"It seems a little odd to be dressing for dinner, doesn't it?" Maude perched on Lucy's enormous four poster bed and fiddled with her bracelet. She had abandoned the backless confection in favor of a more demure mauve gown with full sleeves and a high neckline in recognition of the bereavement. Her restless fidgeting contrasted sharply with the calm, restful figure in front of her.

"It certainly does, but one can't stop eating surely, if one's extremely unpleasant host pops off?" Lucy brushed her hair again, turning a sleek blonde head toward Maude.

"Ever the practical Luce! Anyway, who do you think did it?"

Lucy turned from the mirror and heaved a sigh. "Do you know? I actually started making a list this afternoon just before that policeman came in to start asking me all those questions. I suppose he wasn't half bad, though he did ask a few awkward questions during the whole thing."

Maude blushed and, suddenly finding her bracelet extremely interesting, said softly, "He's rather nice, don't you think? He—I told him he could call me Maude, you know."

"Very nice. Actually, I thought him extremely intelligent too." Lucy could see the blush climbing rosily up Maude's cheeks but chose not to say anything. The inspector was quite nice indeed, and she had found him to be sharp and perceptive—perhaps even a little too perceptive.

"But Maude, it has to be one of us, you know. And he's bound to find out who."

"Can't we do something, Luce? To show him it's not Marty or Biff I mean. Or Julie of course. And Arthur—too ghastly if it were him, don't you think? But then I don't think Harris would actually kill someone! And Garth doesn't seem to have it in him, does he?"

Lucy burst out laughing. "So whom would you propose, you goose? Us?! You've just eliminated all of the suspects!"

Maude smiled, but went on seriously. "Do you have that list? We could try and do a little deduction of our own. After all, we know these people. Rex doesn't. And we were right on the spot!"

Judiciously ignoring the "Rex," Lucy went over to the desk and fished out her notebook.

"Alright, here we are. I'll fill in this list as we go along. I've already started a bit. Anything I'm missing?"

Peering over her shoulder, Maude said "Oh! Put in that Arthur was going to have a drink with Reginald—although I don't know if he ever did. And put down that Julie gave Reginald his coffee. Didn't she? I forget exactly who was milling around."

"And you saw Biff coming up the stairs at night, didn't you?"

"Yes—he looked like he had something in his hand. Maybe a glass of whiskey? I couldn't be sure. But I'm sure he couldn't possibly have done it. Come on, Luce, you know that! And besides, Rex knows about that already and he said it didn't matter in the least," said Maude, a little inaccurately.

"Yes, but if we're to do this, we need to be complete. And the odd thing is, when he and Marty were talking—I was in the library, you know—"

"Yes, being a complete and utter rotter, leaving me with Harris!"

"It's good for you to finally give him the toss instead of just going about it in a roundabout fashion," Lucy said severely. "Live up to that disastrously frank attitude you seem to have around most other people. Anyway, when I was in the library—giving you the opportunity to send Harris about his business—Marty and Biff had the oddest little chat ever! Marty seemed so worried—about Biff and Julie, I should imagine. I'm sure she knew they both could have done it. Though I did find it surprising she thought Biff especially *would* have done it! But Biff told her he had been hanging about with Arthur and Harris in the library. Doesn't square with what you saw, does it?"

"You...you really think..." Maude's brilliant eyes dimmed a little as she contemplated the prospect of a friend committing a murder.

"I don't think anything of the sort. What I do think is we should be complete if we're going to set ourselves up as detectives! I'm sure your Re—Inspector—" Lucy amended hurriedly, "wouldn't go about things in such a slipshod fashion. Let's start with us, shall we? Just to be proper. And then we can go on to everybody else here."

*Lucy Belling and Maude Grimsworth:*
- *Means: Knew where rat poison was.*
- *Motive: None.*
- *Opportunity: None—saw where rat poison was kept but accompanied by others all evening sine then, did not hand anything to RT all evening, did not see him alone.*

*Marty Hemming:*
- *Means: Knew where rat poison was.*
- *Motive: Cut out of will? Biff's business troubles? Any other domestic troubles?*
- *Opportunity: Took RT glass of milk. Worried about something.*

*Biff Hemming:*
- *Means: Knew where rat poison was.*
- *Motive: Business troubles? Marty cut out of will?*
- *Opportunity: Took glass of whiskey upstairs and lied to Marty about it.*

*Julie Bosworth:*
- *Means: Entered terrace during discussion of rat poison location. Did she hear?*
- *Motive: Cut out of will? Wants to marry Garth. Fight in conservatory. Engagement off? Doesn't like RT.*
- *Opportunity: Gave RT coffee, but in conservatory after coffee only.*

*Arthur Pendleton:*
- *Means: Entered terrace during discussion of rat poison location. Did he hear?*
- *Motive: Cut out of will?*
- *Opportunity: Drink w/ RT after dinner?*

*Garth Ashford:*
- *Means: Entered terrace during discussion of rat poison location. Did he hear?*
- *Motive: Fiancée Julie cut out of will?*
- *Opportunity: Tried to give RT cocktail, didn't succeed. Did not see RT alone after. Was in conservatory with Julie after coffee only.*

*Harris Witting:*
- *Means: Was on terrace during discussion of rat poison location. Did he hear?*
- *Motive: None. Seemed afraid of RT? Possibly just thought him rude.*
- *Opportunity: Came down to cocktails behind M & L, did not give RT anything (arrived too late to give him anything at cocktails, never close to him after), did not see him alone.*

Lucy set down her pen. "Phew! That leads us exactly nowhere—unless we're setting out to prove Marty, Biff or Julie did it! Looks rather murky, doesn't it? I do wish we could pin it on someone we didn't care much about. Not that I care a tick for Julie, but Marty and Biff do."

"To be honest, I wouldn't very much mind if it turned out to be Garth. He's not quite right for Julie, is he? And after what we heard last night—I wonder if he *is* after her for the money?"

"Do you know, Maude, something's tickling at the back of my mind about him and that conversation—or fight—he had with Julie. But I can't quite seem to fix on what."

"Seemed like a lover's quarrel to me."

"Yes—but something about the way he said something. I don't know. Something seemed a bit odd."

"*He's* a bit odd. And definitely not quite right for Julie. I wonder what she sees in him? A bit too slick for me, and always has some snarky response."

"To each her own, eh, Maudie? Not all of us can fall for upstanding, law abiding characters, you know..." Lucy suggested slyly, catching Maude's eyes in the mirror as she stowed away the notebook again.

"Luce! You beast!" Tossing a pillow her way and yet with a smile, Maude headed to the door. "Come on, or we'll be the last ones down."

# A FAMILY AFFAIR

"Hello, gentlemen." Biff entered and softly closed the door to the library behind him. "I trust you've been well taken care of? Do you need anything?"

"Nothing, sir, thank you. It's very kind of you to make your home available to us like this. Most unpleasant business. We just want to chat with you and your wife and niece, then we'll be out of your hair for tonight. Although if you would, please let your guests know they should not leave Timberly at present."

"Oh—oh of course, of course. But need you speak with Marty and Julie tonight? I know Marty is completely done in. And Julie was upset. Most upset. I'm not certain she's up, actually. The doctor—I wasn't overly happy when I heard he'd talked Marty into inviting him here, but thank goodness he did come! A good fellow, solid sort of chap. I think he gave her some powders actually."

"Dr. Witting assured us his patient would be up and feeling much more the thing by the evening, sir. And we do like to get impressions while they're fresh, you know. Of course, you're welcome to stay while we speak with Lady Hemming and Miss Bosworth."

"Oh—oh surely—well I don't think that would be necessary, really, but if you think it advisable, of course. Is there anything in particular I can tell you?" Biff sat down across from the inspector and placed his large hands on his knees, leaning forward toward Harte.

"I'd just like some background, sir. When did you and Lady Hemming start living here at Timberly with Lady

Hemming's father? And what brought on the move?"

"I think it's coming up on two years now! Imagine that..."
Biff seemed to lose himself in musing over this, and seemed
startled when Harte cleared his throat to bring him back.
"Yes, yes, two years. Well, you see, I was in a bit of a spot. A
business deal had fallen through a bit. You know how it is.
One of my partners—but not his fault, really, he couldn't
have known it wasn't a sure thing. He had his information
from a close friend—a school friend of his, he said. Well
that's neither here nor there. It was a bit of a tight spot, and
Reginald very kindly offered to have us live here with him.
He might have been a little lonely, don't you know? Well,
we've been here ever since. We rub along quite well. Did. We
used to rub along quite well I should say." Biff paused again,
looking a little bewildered at having to use the past tense, and
staring forlornly at his large soft hands. He took them off his
knees and slowly clasped them in his lap.

Wondering if he truly believed everything had been
chugging along smoothly—all evidence and other witness
testimonies to the contrary—or if this was an act, Hart
looked up at him sharply, his brows drawing close.

"And would you say you or your wife—or your niece—
had any disagreements with Lord Timberly?"

"Oh no! Not at all! Well, I mean, little household things,
you know. But that's bound to happen when you've got
separate personalities living together. But no, not really. Oh
you're thinking perhaps of him calling his lawyer to change
his will. Just a misunderstanding, you know. Reginald
would've come around eventually. They did love each other
you know. I mean—just look at Julie! So upset, poor child.
And of course it had nothing to do with me. Marty has always
been her father's support, so of course, even if he said it, I
really don't believe Reginald would have cut her out. And I
know Marty certainly never thought so."

Following along this tack, it quickly became evident Biff
would not be spilling anything but thickheaded and oblivious
platitudes. He only said that after coffee he had joined the

fellows in the library for a short while—he wasn't sure how long—and had retired upstairs to his dressing room afterward, where he had read for an hour or more before turning in. Although he certainly appeared to be as kind as everyone had previously mentioned, Harte decided he could dispense with further kindly platitudes and soon asked Biff to ask Lady Hemming to come to the library.

As the door closed behind him, Maddock looked with some disgust at his notes. "Nothing! You'd think they were all as gormless as wee chicks! Seems like nobody and nothing would've wanted to kill off that Lord Timberly to hear him tell it!"

"But do you know, Maddock, I thought he was rather hiding something. Or at least he was worried. Did you see how he kept talking about how Miss Bosworth loved her grandfather and was so upset about his death? You'd think the two had been bosom pals instead of only having been reacquainted in the past two years. And none too fondly, I might add! I'll tell you what—get Maitland on to him and see what sort of things he's been involved in, will you? If there's any whiff of fraud or fishy business dealings he'll know about it. And let's see if Lady Hemming has anything to add. I must say, I can't quite see either her or his lordship poisoning someone in cold blood, can you? But perhaps she'll let something spill about her niece that Lord Hemming wouldn't."

\*

Marty entered the library accompanied by Lucy. "I—I do hope it's alright, Inspector. It's not that—I mean to say—it's because—"

As Marty got lost in a series of half sentences, Harte won Lucy's approval by nodding kindly and saying, "Quite so, ma'am. Do come and sit, won't you? Miss Belling is welcome to stay, and I shall try my best not to be a complete nuisance."

Glancing a bit wildly into his eyes, Marty seemed to calm down as she took in his assured air and kind words. Settling herself in a shuffle of scarves and frilled skirts, she took Lucy's hand, saying, "I'm ready—let's begin" as though facing an inquisitor.

"I'd just like you to tell me a little about Lord Timberly, how you and your husband happened to move here, just some background, you know. And then perhaps a little bit more about yesterday in particular that will help us pin down everyone's movements."

"Father is—was—always a little short-tempered. I was always a little worried about him, living as he was, all alone here. And when he asked us to come live here—well, well—" looking at Lucy for encouragement, Marty plunged on, "it was actually quite a godsend to us, you know. Biff isn't—well he hasn't had the best luck in business. So the timing was wonderful. But he always got along with Father. And Father wasn't really very easy to get along with—but Biff can get along with anyone!"

"And Miss Bosworth?"

"Oh Julie! Julie—well—Julie loved her grandfather. Not—that is to say, they weren't—well she didn't know him too well after all. She always came to us in the holidays after my dear sister died, you know. But of course she's out of school now anyway, and has a flat up in London—quite unsuitable, but what can you do. Girls these days. Although of course, Lucy darling, you and Maude are so much more grown-up, don't you think? Even though you're almost the same age."

Lucy pressed her hand and said calmly, "Yes of course. But do you think the inspector wants to know that, Marty?"

"Oh! Of course! Well. Well Julie hasn't visited much, so of course she can't know her grandfather really. But she loved him, I'm sure of it. I mean—I mean, that's why she's so upset, of course."

Maddock, glancing up, saw his superior scrutinizing not Lady Hemming, as he had expected, but Miss Belling instead. Being seated as he was behind the two women, Maddock couldn't see the inscrutable look that had interested Harte so much.

"Just so, ma'am. And Mr. Ashford? Have he and Miss Bosworth been engaged for long?"

"Oh no, no. I don't think—well, I don't really know, to tell you the truth. I'm sure—well I'm sure he'll be fine, and I'm sure he had nothing to do with this whole business. This is the first time we're meeting him, you know, although I do think Julie has mentioned him a number of times in the past couple of months."

"And could you tell me a little about yesterday evening, Lady Hemming? Perhaps you could describe the evening following dinner?"

"Well Father went up rather early, you know. He always did. I can't say he was grumbling more than usual, although—" Marty's face had a stricken look on it "—he did complain about the food and—and—" she raised a shaking hand to her ashen lips.

"Marty don't take on so, there's a dear. You know it had nothing to do with the food, and whenever he was poisoned, you couldn't have prevented it."

"Yes. Yes, he must have been poisoned before coffee, of course. That's why he was complaining—complaining rather a lot, actually, now I think about it." Marty opened her mouth to say something more, reconsidered, and shut it with a snap.

"Do you know when the rest of the party retired?"

"I came up when Maude and Lucy did—around eleven wasn't it?" glancing to Lucy for confirmation, Marty continued, "And Biff came up shortly after. I hadn't fallen asleep yet, and he came straight to bed. I heard him come up the stairs and everything."

Lucy studiously avoided Harte's gaze, trying not to let it show on her face just how surprised and disappointed she was that Marty had omitted telling the inspector about taking Reginald's nightly cocoa up to him. Unwanted suspicion flickered across her mind. It was all she could do to keep a straight face.

Harte, meanwhile, was equally anxious to avoid Lucy's too-discerning eye. Being careful not to let his skepticism show, he merely let Marty continue in this strain for a few minutes, thanked her, and asked her to send Julie in. He sat back contemplating the door as it shut behind them.

*

Miss Julie Bosworth did not look like she had spent the day crying for her dead grandfather. Her blonde hair was beautifully curled and dressed, her lips shaded deep red, her eyelashes blackened, and her brows perfectly done. The impeccably applied make-up could not, however, hide the very real paleness of her cheeks, and no amount of mascara would distract the viewer from the worry haunting her eyes. She entered alone, pausing theatrically at the doorway until she was sure both Harte and Maddock's eyes were trained upon her. With a great show of putting away a delicate lace handkerchief, she entered slowly into the library on staggeringly high heels.

Depositing herself gracefully in the proffered chair and practically lounging, Julie asked, "You wanted to see me, Inspector? I can't imagine what I should be able to tell you."

Harte could not know from her voice how valiantly Julie was trying to hold on to the languid pose she had adopted the previous day. He heard only a put-on affectation with the veriest tremor underneath the whole construct.

"I am sorry for your loss. It must have been a shock."

"Oh. Yes. Of course."

"However, it must be a comfort to you to be with your loved ones at a time like this."

Julie merely gave a little nod at this.

"If you would, could you tell me a little about your grandfather and your—er—" Harte paused for an instant and continued with a doubtful hint, "—Mr. Ashford?"

The hunted look deepened. "My grandfather—was—he was not, perhaps quite taken with my—with—with Mr.

Ashford. But he would have understood eventually, there was no—they were cordial with each other."

Harte questioned her about the previous day coaxingly, receiving no new information as he had expected, but slowly leading her along her narrative. She gave him an unvarnished and slightly bored account of the previous evening. She had come to tea in Garth's company, they were not there when the discussion of rat poison took place. She had had a headache because of the thunder. After tea she and Garth had gone into the house for a while before going upstairs to dress for dinner. They had come down for cocktails. They were not the last ones there, though she couldn't say who had been there and who hadn't. Dinner was uneventful except for the spilled wine. By the time everyone gathered for coffee she had decided her grandfather was just being crotchety, perhaps because of his gout. She had taken it upon herself to make amends and taken a cup of coffee to her grandfather. He didn't seem in the mood to make up, so she had given up. That was the last she saw of him. During this narrative Julie seemed to let down her guard and relaxed once again into her usual languid pauses. Harte chose his moment and changed tack a little.

"When did you meet Mr. Ashford? Through mutual acquaintances?"

"I—we met at a party, a few—two months—ago."

"A whirlwind romance, in fact."

"No, no, nothing like that. I—we met at a friend's party. Garth was there to paint her portrait and we just hit it off."

"And when did you and Mr. Ashford marry?"

Startled out of her lounging pose, Julie sat bolt upright, her eyes widening. The effect of a frightened rabbit made Harte feel uncomfortably like a snake about to attack the helpless creature.

"I—I—you can't—how did you—no! We're not!"

"Miss Bosworth, or shall I say, Mrs. Ashford, I think I should warn you, as of this moment, your husband, Mr. Garth Ashford, finds himself in an extremely grave position, and even more, so do you. You arrived here, secretly married, trying to cajole your grandfather into changing his mind about cutting you out of his will unless you married Mr. Pendleton. Finding it impossible to move him and understanding that his lawyer's arrival—and his changing of the will—were imminent, you or Mr. Ashford—or possibly both—plotted to poison your grandfather and end his life before he could change his will. You both heard where the poison was kept, you handed the coffee to your grandfather, and both your movements yesterday evening are shrouded with secrecy. You yourself do not care to give me a clear account of your movements, nor did Mr. Ashford. I should advise you very strongly to think clearly before you deny your marriage or to tell me any more lies."

Harte's flinty voice cut through the tense atmosphere and his eyes snapped cold and sharp. Julie, sapped of all her strength, cowered in her chair and burst into loud sobs. The persona of the fashionable young lady dissolved in her tears, revealing a frightened, shaken young girl.

"I want my Aunt Marty! I want my Aunt Marty!"

At a sign from Harte, Maddock went off in search of Marty, returning shortly with a little coterie consisting of Marty, Biff, Lucy, and Maude.

Although resigned to having an audience, Harte was still startled to be faced with an avenging angel in the wild-haired Marty who turned on him now.

"Oh my poor child! My poor, poor child! What are they doing to you? I told them you were too weak still, you can't stand up to this." Marty turned on Harte, pointing an accusing finger at him. "You! You can see she's weak, and yet you hound her, harass her until she has a breakdown!"

Affronted at these accusations and feeling it provident to stop the farce, Harte interrupted her torrent with his cool, quiet voice.

"I'm afraid, ma'am, I only asked about Mrs. Ashford's husband and warned her of the dangerous position they find themselves in."

# DISCLOSURES

At Detective Inspector Harte's words, a shocked silence fell over the room, interrupted only by soft sobs from Julie's chair. Marty halted in the middle of an acrimonious sentence and gaped as though struck by lightning. Biff's eyes grew to the size of extra large lemon drops. Maude and Lucy gripped each other's hands, exchanging wide-eyed glances that spoke volumes.

Finding her tongue first, Maude turned an incredulous face to Julie and asked, "Is it true? Why didn't you say?! Have you been lying to us this whole time?"

Stung back to life by these words, Marty flung an arm around her niece and said rather wildly, "Of course not! Julie would never—would never—" her voice faltered as her niece's shoulders shook in silent sobs but no denial arrived.

It was only many minutes later, when Marty had covered Julie in hugs and embraces, half-finished sentences and flustered encouragements, and when Biff had placed a calming hand on his niece's shoulders and said quietly that of course they would be there for her no matter what, that Julie's sobs slowed and eventually stopped.

Raising a teary face to the inspector, she breathed raggedly and said in a much more normal and unaffected voice, "It's true." Holding on to Marty's hand in her lap and hooking her fingers through Biff's large hand on her shoulder, she continued, "I—we—were married a month ago. It was a bit of a whirlwind affair. I knew it was going to be a no-go with Arthur, and he was already dangling after some floozy he'd picked up somewhere, although I'm sure I don't care, and not that I did then either. But of course Garth was so nice, and one does like to feel as if—as if—well, I knew he loved me. At least, I thought so. No matter what Grandpapa said about people only wanting to marry me for my money. With all the things Garth said, and Arthur being so horrible, and Garth was ever so nice to begin with. We were married in a civil ceremony. And oh, it was awful. I never even had a wedding dress! And no gifts either! And I couldn't call any friends or tell anyone!" Having long discarded the lacy patch of cotton she had used to dab at her eyes, Julie now started bawling all over Biff's large and eminently more useful, if not quite ladylike, handkerchief.

Maude felt it prudent, at this point, to avoid catching Lucy's eye. She had a bad habit of having the most inappropriate reactions to serious situations, and she could already feel a wayward chuckle bubbling up. Although it was really too bad for Julie, of course, and poor Marty and Biff would be saddled with Garth forever as well, keeping a straight face over these astounding disclosures was almost too much to ask. They had known there was once something between Arthur and Julie and that things hadn't quite turned out well, but for Julie to go off and marry the first flattering painter she came across just because he was "nice" was just a hair too ridiculous to ignore.

Lucy, meanwhile, stared at the carved sandalwood cigarette box sitting on the table in an effort to avoid Maude's eye. She had been with Maude in too many awkward situations to risk a loud guffaw from that damsel at this delicate stage in the proceedings. Lucy privately wondered whether Arthur had heaved a sigh of relief when Julie took up with Garth, or whether he was still caught up with her in some way. One didn't drop the love of one's life for a "floozy" surely? But then again, there always seemed to be an odd tension between Arthur and Julie. He had obviously cut things off with Julie at some point, and Lucy found herself hoping he wasn't the sort to pine over a girl who would marry someone else in a fit of pique. The fact that Julie seemed to be more upset about the lack of a huge wedding where she could show off in front of Arthur rather than the fact that she had married a rackety painter only made Lucy think perhaps Julie and Garth deserved each other.

Raising red-rimmed eyes, Julie choked out, "I'm so sorry. I—I did want you to be present, Marty and Biff. But Garth wouldn't hear of it, said we'd surprise you!"

"Darling, you know we love you. But why the cloak-and-dagger stuff? Did you really have to rush into it? You know we would have supported you no matter what." Marty spoke in a tender voice.

"I know. It's just—Garth thought it better this way. I should have realized then he wasn't—he didn't—that there was something fishy. But I was so caught up in it all. It was only after we got married that I started realizing he didn't really have—have that much of a caché, as he'd said he did. He mainly got by doing miniature work and a few portraits here and there. He started being so insistent we come down here and get Grandpapa to settle some money on us. Saying he knew how it would be, that I'd trapped him..."

"Trapped him! Why the little—"

"But I did, I did!" Julie said in a wretched voice. "I told him I would inherit so much money, never told him how much Grandpapa disliked the idea of me marrying anybody but Arthur. And Arthur was being such a snake then, too, and not caring an ounce. Not that I care!" Julie gave a little toss of her head and burst into tears again.

"I don't know what to do! I never thought—I never thought Garth would, would—how could he! Oh I knew he wasn't happy when Grandpapa said he was calling in Jellaby, but I never, ever thought—oh but he did, he did! He must have! And now I'm married to him and I can never be free! And I'm sure Arthur isn't with that floozy anymore and maybe he just needed a little time! And what's the point of being married if I couldn't even tell anybody." Her shoulders sagged as though they carried the weight of the world on them. Julie leaned into Marty and proceeded to drench all her aunt's many scarves with mascara-tinted tears.

Feeling there was little new information to be got and that the scene had gone on too long, Harte judiciously shepherded the little trio—aunt, uncle, and niece—out of the room. He heaved a soft sigh of relief as the door shut behind them. Harte seemed to have forgotten Miss Belling and Miss Grimsworth were still in the room, but came to with a jerk upon hearing Maude's bell-like tones.

"Well! To think she's been married the whole time! The little stinker!"

"Miss Grimsworth, Miss Belling—"

"Oh do let us stay! We have a whole slew of important things and insights and such to share with you, and I know we'll be so very helpful! Besides, I couldn't possibly go out into the hall and not shout out to everyone that Julie married the painter to spite Arthur and she didn't even get a wedding dress out of it!"

Harte found himself smiling at this and felt it impossible to shoo Maude and Lucy out. Maddock stared woodenly at his notebook as Detective Inspector Harte considered the highly improper and extremely irregular request. The sergeant was not altogether surprised when Harte nodded slowly, and invited both ladies to have a seat on the comfortable leather banquette and took a seat across from them in a chair embossed with brass buttons. Not for nothing had the inspector risen meteorically in the force. Of course the war had created spaces for talented young men to come up in the ranks faster than they otherwise would, but that wasn't all. Harte was known for his less than regular methods and his unconventional ways with witnesses and evidence were only overlooked because he always seemed to present a solution nobody else could have possibly found. In the Billsley case it had been his willingness to listen to an impish nine-year-old's testimony—littered as it was with half-truths and imaginary doings—that led him to the cat burglar who had made off with jewels worth thousands. And it was only because he had succeeded in running to ground a retired butler who had confided in him about the doings of his former employers that the Cholmondley case had cracked. He'd been known to deviate from the book in search of answers before. Of course, so far his irregularities had not concerned a striking young female with a certain air and a sparkle in her eyes that seemed to attract the inspector a bit overmuch according to his sergeant. Maddock chose to overlook this departure from the norm, stoically believing in the phrase he had heard his childhood teacher utter, "*que sera sera.*" After all, the inspector knew his own job best, and it wasn't the sergeant's place— and more than his head was worth—to go telling him how to go about it. Maddock himself took an unobtrusive seat a little removed from the small group.

For a few moments, Harte merely looked at the two young women seated across from him, Miss Belling in an asymmetrical navy silk crepe dress with a string of jet beads coming down to her waist, and Maude in a pale chiffon confection with long floating sleeves and a single gold strand around her neck. Lucy's shoe tapped a little tune against the legs of the circular wooden table separating them. A brief smile passed over the inspector's face as he looked into Maude's blue-grey eyes. He noticed they now seemed more a deep shade of violet, brought out by the mauve of her soft dress, and were sparkling with suppressed excitement, curiosity, and that ever-present hint of laughter. Encountering Miss Belling's grave brown eyes, he turned serious once again. It was Miss Belling who spoke first.

"I don't imagine we have anything much more substantive to add that you haven't found out yourself, of course. But Maude and I were chatting about this investigation and thought..." Lucy paused, looking up at the inspector uncertainly. Making up her mind, she went on in her reassuring voice. "You probably have all the information you could get out of everybody you've met. In fact, you've managed to get a sight more than we or Marty or Biff could have hoped for," she added wryly. "But Maude and I made a little list last night, and we'd like to share it with you, just in case it helps. We've been listening to everyone, but so far the only people who have been acting strange or—or otherwise out of the ordinary have been Julie and Garth. I think it's fairly evident Julie thinks that Garth—well, she's rather upset. I can't believe she would kill her own grandfather. But there you are." Lucy handed over the little list to Harte.

A moment later, as Harte was still perusing the list, Maude impatiently jumped in. "Rex—Inspector—it wasn't Marty or Biff, we know that. You don't have to believe us of course, but we know them so well. Neither one of them would hurt a fly. If there's anything at all we can do to help you only have to ask!"

He looked up, nodding slowly. "Thank you for this list. It does have a point or two that didn't come out, and I'm grateful. Unfortunately I can't quite take you into the case, as you must know. But if you would only keep your eyes and ears open, I can assure you I will always be quite willing to listen. But please," Harte looked directly at Maude, turned to include Lucy as well, and said, "you mustn't put yourself forward or let it be known you may be inclined to search for clues or trying to solve this puzzle yourselves. It could be dangerous. We know when someone has killed once, the second time is easier, and I—" his eyes met Maude's again, "—would hate to have you put yourself in harm's way."

As a rosy blush stole up Maude's cheeks, Lucy answered for both of them. "We'll keep that in mind. Come, Maude. We've bothered the inspector enough for now. I'm sure he has his investigations to carry out." And the two walked out of the library, leaving Harte looking once again at the sheet of paper in his hands.

"Maddock—take a look at this. Does anything pop out?"

Taking the sheet of paper gingerly, Maddock looked at it once, then again. His large eyes swiveled toward the inspector. "I'm sorry sir, not immediately, I don't see anything. Unless you're thinking this Garth fellow did have a chance to go into the conservatory and was there with Miss— Mrs. Ashford. But when did he give the old fellow the poison then? I don't quite see this old curmudgeon hopping out of bed to let in that fellow for a nightcap, do you?"

"No...no, I don't...then again..."

"But he might for his granddaughter, sir."

"But is it possible? You know, Maddock, for some reason I think this little list Miss Grimsworth and Miss Belling have presented us with is vital. But I can't for the life of me think why. I think I'd like to see those notes of yours typed up as soon as possible and see if it all fits together. And I believe we'll have Lord and Lady Hemming in again for a question or two. At the moment it looks rather grim for—"

A sharp knock sounded on the door, and a moment later the knob twisted, letting in the ever-debonair figure of Arthur Pendleton.

"My apologies, gentlemen. I hope I haven't interrupted any cozy tête-à-têtes? I deduced, from the servants, of course, that you seem to have found out Miss Julie Bosworth is in fact Mrs. Garth Ashford. In light of the fact, and deducing further—" Arthur gave a dry smile, "that attention would of course shift to her as a suspect, I have come to amend my statement. I remembered I had left out a little portion of yesterday evening, which I feel would be vital knowledge for you."

Harte curtly nodded him over to a chair and asked him to take a seat.

"No, no, no need, really. I just wanted to clarify the little time discrepancy the charming Dr. Witting pointed out. I did in fact step out of the room for a little while not, as I suggested earlier, merely to go to the cloakroom. In fact, I saw Mr. Ashford heading rather wildly from the conservatory up the stairs with his glass of whiskey in his hands. A nightcap for himself, no doubt. I went in to investigate and found Miss—" a look of distaste crossed Arthur's face. "You'll have to forgive me—an old habit, you know. I found Julie was crying in there. I tried to comfort her. It appears she had had rather an acrimonious dispute with her—with Mr. Ashford. She calmed down after a while, and went upstairs, aiming straight for bed. That is all, really."

"Indeed, sir? And you only choose to tell us this now?"

"I had some misplaced concerns for the lady's honor, of course. Lest you misinterpret my actions," Arthur said delicately, an urbane smile upon his lips again.

Giving him a sharp look, Harte nodded once again. "And you've come to amend your statement because you now see it would behoove her?"

"Rather, I should say I thought it expedient to tell you what I had remembered."

"Is that all?"

"All."

"Thank you, sir. I think we shall have to consider your statement very carefully."

Arthur gave a little bow and retreated through the door again. Harte turned to Maddock and raised his eyebrows until they disappeared into his thick brown hair.

"Lies, damn lies, or—the truth?"

"It's my thinking Mr. City Smart there realized his lady love would find herself in some hot water if it came out she was married. I wonder if he's still smitten with her? I don't see how he can have known Lord Timberly met his demise before midnight, but if what he says is true, it means Miss Julie didn't have any time to go upstairs and poison her grandfather until at least half past midnight—half an hour after he must have died at the latest. In fact, sir..." Maddock continued laboriously, "he can't know the estimated time of death. While he's given Miss Julie an alibi—and created an opportunity for Mr. Garth—that's again if Lord Timberly would have admitted him to his room late at night, which isn't something as he'd do in my mind at least—he might have struck it out for himself."

Harte sighed and ran a hand through his well-ordered cropped curls, but only said "Get Lord and Lady Hemming once again, will you? And see if you can scrounge up a cup of tea for us."

# SUSPICION

"Lord Hemming, Lady Hemming, please, do be seated." Harte nodded graciously and took up a seat across from them. Marty still wore the scarf bespattered with Julie's mascara-laden tears. Her fingers were rapidly unraveling its soft blue wool. What started as a worrying at a loose strand now threatened to unwind the long, slim scarf in its entirety. Her hair was in its habitual disarray, the inspector noted, and she seemed a little too eager to help.

"Of course, of course. We're distraught, of course, by Julie's news, but then—children—young love—you know what young girls are like!"

Detective Inspector Harte tried to smile wisely and look older than his years, as though he did indeed know what young girls were like. In his mind, however, the sardonic thought occurred that less flighty young things than Miss Julie—Maude and Miss Belling popped to mind—might have considered a little more before rushing precipitately into such folly.

"We're glad to help in any way, Inspector. Aren't we, darling?"

Harte wondered if the look she cast at her husband really did have that much despair in it or if he was reading too much into one glance.

Biff, meanwhile, sat looking at his large hands, absently clasped in his lap. He looked up at his wife, slowly moved his gaze toward the inspector, and sat up a little straighter. "Of course, darling. Of course, Inspector. We are happy to help of course." Having made what he felt to be a sufficient contribution to the conversation, he retreated into the background to let his more voluble wife take the stage.

"Although of course I can't quite imagine what you might have to ask us. We've told you everything, you know, absolutely everything. And it's quite horrified us. Father—oh I can't even bear to think of it. But of course, you know, he angered many people. I shouldn't wonder at it if someone had broken in. I mean to say, you do hear such things about raving lunatics and all that. And there's an asylum quite close by, I believe. Although of course there haven't been any news reports, have there? But I must say, Jennings should really make sure he's locked up well. I must have a word with him. But the servants, you know, so trusted—and so upset by all this, I need hardly say. Quite upset. I've already had a maid or two wanting to leave already. But that's silly of course, who would kill them after all..."

Marty seemed to run out of steam as Harte merely regarded her silently. After a moment he spoke in a quiet voice.

"Who would kill your father, ma'am? That's the question we're here to find the answer to."

"Of—of course..."

Biff surprised Harte by speaking up. "My wife is just upset, Inspector. This whole experience has been rather harrowing for her."

Turning his attention to Biff, Harte said in the same measured voice, "I hope you will be able to help me, then, to clear it up a little. I'm sure the sooner we find answers the sooner we can bring this harrowing episode to a close."

Biff looked at Harte with an indiscernible light in his eyes and reached over to take one of Marty's hands in his.

"Lord Hemming—once again, could you go into your own movements after dinner yesterday? I'd just like some clarification on what you did after the ladies, that is to say, Miss Grimsworth, Miss Belling and your wife, went upstairs."

"He came right up, Inspector. Not too long after me, actually. I was falling asleep, of course, but of course I knew he had come up and so on. It was just shortly after we came up. Not at all enough time—not very long, in fact." Marty stopped in a hurry.

"Not enough time, Lady Hemming? For what?"

"What? Oh you do catch me in my words. I—" Marty's knuckles turned white as her grip on Biff's hand tightened. Harte saw him hide a wince, but he answered calmly enough.

Lord Hemming's eyes, usually a warm chocolate, acquired a hard sheen as he spoke. "As I told you earlier, Inspector, I spent some time with Arthur and Harris in the library. They seemed inclined to stay up chatting, so I made my way upstairs. I retired to my dressing room. It is next to my wife's, which might have been why she heard me come upstairs. I read for an hour or so, then went to bed."

"Biff!"

Ignoring, for the moment, Lady Hemming's distressed cry, Harte pressed on. "When exactly did you go upstairs, sir? And how long would you say you stayed talking with Mr. Pendleton and Dr. Witting?"

"I'm not sure. It could have been ten minutes, it could have been thirty. I did not look at my watch."

"Did you look at your watch when you retired to bed?"

"No, Inspector, I regret to say I did not."

Marty had been steadily shredding her scarf during this exchange, and now began quite literally wringing her hands.

Seeing her reaction, Harte asked her, "And Lady Hemming—could you please describe to me once again Lord Timberly's demeanor when you took his milk upstairs to him?"

It was the first time Harte had seen anyone's jaw actually drop. At his question, Marty's hands stilled completely. After a silence that stretched on for moment after excruciating moment, she said a little breathlessly, "Cocoa—it was cocoa. I always take up his cocoa. Of course, I didn't think anything of it when I went up with the cocoa." With a half-scared, half-defiant look she went on, "I take up his cocoa every night. I—I don't suppose I mentioned it earlier—how clever of you to find out. But of course one forgets these little habits. I—my father—he did complain of feeling a little ill but I thought nothing of it then, but that shows, doesn't it, that he must have been poisoned rather earlier in the evening? Not at coffee or—or—after?"

"Unfortunately, I can't reassure you on that point."

His response threw both Lord and Lady Hemming into a deep silence. Marty's hands returned to their worrying, and Biff sat staring at the desk from behind which Harte was conducting his interrogation, clasping his hands together in his lap. After a few moments, thinking the silence had gone on too long, Harte tried a different tack.

"You see, Lord Hemming, Lady Hemming, I am only trying to establish your movements to give me a better sense of chronology. Given the poison—strychnine—and the dosage, you must see I have to know who was in contact with Lord Timberly at any point in the evening. I will set aside Lady Hemming's visit with the cocoa for the moment. My questions to you are also in the interest of establishing others' movements over the course of the evening. I have ascertained to my satisfaction Miss Grimsworth and Miss Belling had no connection to Lord Timberly—and therefore no motive. I have no reason to doubt their word when they tell me they went upstairs and to bed at the same time as your wife. In effect, they provide a corroboration of Lady Hemming's movements. It's not that I don't believe you. In fact, the opposite. I have every desire to believe you. It's just that Miss Julie and Mr. Ashford's movements—"

Before Harte could finish his sentence, Biff jumped out of his seat, roaring, "My niece had nothing to do with this! You leave her alone, you understand? You've already upset her enough! I won't have this—this badgering nonsense under this roof! I absolutely forbid it!" His eyes flashed and it was only Lady Hemming's wrenching grip on his arm that stopped him from lunging at the inspector. Biff's face was turning alarmingly purple, and his voice, unaccustomed to shouting, ended on a crack. His stance reminded Harte of a pomeranian confronting a bulldog, barking and growling, with hackles raised, ready to launch itself into a fight despite knowing it would be bested in one swipe.

Detective Inspector Harte met the older man's gaze unflinchingly. His voice had steel in it when he answered. "Please, sir. I must ask you to take a seat once again. We are not making any accusations. And it won't help your niece's cause to have you jump to her defense quite so quickly. At the moment she is not under suspicion, but seeing her near and dear family members so quick to believe she might be implicated is something to take note of."

At this Biff subsided like a deflated balloon. The air went out of him all of a sudden and he turned back into the mild-mannered, rather absent-minded, middle-aged man Harte had grown accustomed to. His eyes lost their fire and became dull. Marty, who had been clinging to his arm during his outburst put her own arms around him and sobbed, "Oh Biff, oh Biff! Don't worry, darling, they can't—they won't—she didn't do it, you know, don't worry."

Turning to Harte with a teary face, Marty said, "She couldn't have done it. Oh no. I—I did take my father his cocoa while everyone was upstairs. He seemed quite alright. Just grumbling. The food didn't suit him, he said. And his gout. And Biff—I didn't hear him come up the stairs, but, but—Maude told me she saw him come up their stairs with a glass of whiskey in his hands. He didn't see Lord Reginald, I know he didn't—tell them, Biff, oh tell them, do!"

All the force gone out of his voice, Biff responded softly. "I did come up about ten or fifteen minutes after Marty and the girls had gone upstairs. I poured myself a splash of whiskey and came up the other side of the landing, the stairs near Reginald's room. I might have had some notion of going to see him, to discuss this business. Perhaps that's when Maude saw me—I had no idea. But I only paused by Reginald's door. Didn't see or hear anything, either. But I couldn't do it. I—I must admit, I was a bit afraid of his reaction. I went into my dressing room, as I said. But I didn't read. In fact, I saw my valet, Charles, who had just been in—I had rung for him before I went upstairs—and asked him to play cards with me for a while. The poor fellow's sick now, but you can ask him if you want. I don't know how late we stayed up playing cards. I'm afraid I put him in a bit of an awkward situation, really—not really done, you know, playing cards with your master at all hours of night—but I needed something to distract me. Then I went to bed. Must have been around one o'clock. I didn't kill my father-in-law, Inspector. But I also know my wife didn't either, and neither did my niece. She's a sweet child. Perhaps a little lost when it comes to choosing the right man, and I know she didn't get along with her grandfather recently, but she would never kill anybody." Biff subsided after this long speech, his energy spent, his shoulders sagging.

In the meanwhile, Marty had been doing some thinking of her own, and as her husband became quiet, she exclaimed, "Oh! Those—those—how could they! It was Maude and Lucy, wasn't it? They told you? Why would they do that? Why would they—they're our friends! Our dear friends! No, Biff, listen! Only Maude knew you came upstairs with the whiskey. She must have told Lucy because those two never did have secrets from each other. And now they've told the inspector! They've betrayed us! We've been nursing vipers in our bosom!"

Harte found himself more than a little annoyed at this description of Maude as a viper and felt it was unjust to accuse Lucy so as well. He said with some asperity, "I think, Lord and Lady Hemming, we've had as much discussion as we all can handle today. I can only assure you we don't leap to false judgments, and I have no intention of bringing home this crime to someone who did not commit it. I would suggest that instead of keeping what might be important information from the police, you share it candidly in the future."

Maddock rose and bowed out the shattered Lord Hemming and the sobbing Lady Hemming with rare aplomb.

Closing the door with a gentle snap, he turned around to look at the inspector.

Harte rubbed his eyes and wearily glanced at the little ormolu clock on the heavily carved oak mantelpiece across from him. He said, "See if the valet is well enough to give you a brief statement, will you? And then I think it's time you and I packed up here, Maddock. I want to see if there's any response to the wire you sent to Maitland to find out more about the kindly Lord Hemming's business dealings and to see if the Yard has ever had any dealings with him or his business partners. And, since it's going to be a long night of burning the midnight oil for us, comparing all these statements, I propose we get us some dinner. Let's hope the pub down in the village will have something hearty enough to last us out. What with protective uncles and cocoa-giving daughters and ungrateful godsons and granddaughters abounding, I can't see straight for all the motives and opportunities! It's a wonder old Reginald didn't meet his demise sooner. And tomorrow the lawyer is arriving bright and early. I've asked him to stop by the pub first before stopping here, so we'll see him at breakfast before we face this loony bin again."

Harte picked up the list Lucy had handed him once more, turned, and handed it to Maddock. "As you're typing up your notes, see if that fits in, will you? I don't know if I'm turning superstitious in the face of this huge mess, but somehow I believe the answer is written right there, staring us in the face."

# LORD OF THE MANOR

After a rather less than delightful meal, Harte laid his knife down with relief when the waiter came over to tell him he had a telephone call from Scotland Yard. He left Maddock to continue pushing morose and deflated potatoes around what had been billed as a steak but was a closer approximation to a door stop around his plate.

"Harte."

"Hello, sir. It's Maitland. I called earlier, but you were out. I'm calling about the gentleman you asked me to look into."

Harte's ears perked up and he turned inward toward the wall as if to shield the telephone from any unwelcome auditors.

"Well? What'd you find about Lord Hemming and his business dealings? Anything there?"

"Quite a lot I'd say—the fellow hasn't been involved in a single deal that hasn't soured in some extremely dubious fashion over the past twenty years! I've got the feeling we should've been looking into his business dealings a sight earlier than this!"

As Harte listened intently, Maitland went on to describe a series of spectacularly failed investments and deals as well as others that had been snuffed out quietly with nothing more to show than a paper trail that petered out into nothingness. On more than one occasion, other investors had been left out in the cold and in at least one case there was a suicide that could be linked to a disastrous investment brokered by Lord Bartholomew Hemming. Maitland ended by saying he had a man on the way to Timberly with all the papers he had been able to find, and he had a call in to a couple of other offices that might be able to turn up something more.

"You've either got the world's biggest patsy on your hands, or else we've got ourselves a new crook to keep an eye on, sir."

"Thank you, Maitland. I'm glad you had your man take off when he did. He should be reaching in the next hour or so, and I'll be very interested to get my hands on these papers. Did any names pop up often? Any co-investors, I mean to say?"

"In some of his earlier deals his father-in-law seems to have put in a big amount one way or the other. But that seemed to end fairly quickly. Otherwise some of the names are ones you're bound to recognize, sir. Remember James Aldridge and Lord Mullaney who got named in that huge swindle a few years ago? Both've done some business with this fellow. And I have to say, it doesn't look like Hemming got off any too easily with those two. But what's he doing having any dealings at all with that sort of company, is what I want to know. Especially after their names had been splashed all over the news! Must've been something in it."

"And what about recently? There's been some noise about a recent deal of his that fell through."

"The last thing I could get my hands on was last year. I don't know about anything more recent, but might have been an older deal that just went bust. Have any more details for me to go on?"

"Unfortunately, no. Can't get a word out of him or his wife. But it looks like some creditor's found him out and got his hooks into him. See what you can find, will you? And give me a call at any time. I'll keep an eye out for your man. Goodnight."

Harte stood looking at the telephone for a moment or two with a frown on his face. He returned, still frowning, to the table where Maddock had, amazingly, polished off the doorstop and the sad potatoes and was now making his way through a sickly looking pudding.

Glancing at the empty plate in faint disgust even as his own stomach still growled, Harte said "Looks like Hemming might not be quite as foolish and nice as he says he is, Maddock. Maitland's got Gumby on his way with some papers and details about what seems to be rather a dirty business past."

"They did say he's none too smart about business, though, sir."

"Well I'd like to see if he is actually just a patsy, as Maitland put it, or if he's been playing a deeper game all along. Apparently the old man had invested some money with him in the past but nothing recently. Maybe he was trying to put the screw on his father-in-law and the fellow wouldn't budge. Seems to have been fairly hard-headed. And if some old creditor's poking up his head wanting to be paid back, that gives us an excellent motive for knocking off the rich and obstinate father-in-law, don't you think?"

Maddock gave Harte a dubious look and said, "Miss Belling did say he was no good at business, sir."

Harte's stomach gave another growl and he snapped, "I'll thank you not to pick favorites among our witnesses, Maddock. It doesn't do to base anything on what one witness might say. I'm going upstairs to freshen up a bit. Come get me when Gumby arrives."

Harte left Maddock gaping at the unfairness of his statement, eyes wide and mouth flapping open. It was only much later, when he was preparing for bed, that a witty, articulate snub about kettles, pots, Miss Grimsworth and favorites popped into his head. Sadly he couldn't quite bring himself to march out in his pajamas and confront the detective inspector in a state of undress at that hour. At the moment, however, his face merely grew more hake-like, and he felt compelled to abandon what was left of his pudding in outrage and despair.

It was while Maddock was still stewing over Harte's extremely uncalled-for criticism that a trim, bird-like young man walked into the room, his bright eyes sparkling, and an air of suppressed energy making itself felt around him.

"Well if it isn't Homer Maddock! Maitland said you were up here with Harte. Where's the big man then? And how're you keeping yourself amused in this forsaken corner? Took me who knows how long to get out here—been traveling for days, it feels like!"

Cheering up at the sight of one of his peers, Maddock's face grew more animated, and in a few moments even the beginnings of a smile were evident. He and the unfittingly named Gumby were old friends, and ten minutes spent in the company of the sharp little man were enough to put Maddock back into his usual sanguine frame of mind, at which point he remembered they were actually supposed to give the papers Gumby had brought to the detective inspector. These were hailed with much gusto, and the three men fell to sorting through the thick envelope full of odds and ends Inspector Maitland had sent on with his subordinate.

A little while later Harte let out a whistle and tossed the papers he held onto the crooked-legged little desk in his room.

"The man's a fool! Nobody would've put money into Rushmore's mines if he'd had half an eye on the papers!"

"But look at this, sir—the Farnley deal—didn't we pull in Michael Farnley for questioning? But from these papers, it almost looks like it wasn't him at all. Could it have been Hemming behind the whole matter all along?"

Again the men started going through the papers, but this time calling out a deal or an investment they recognized, as well as any information that might show them whether Hemming was really just a dunce at gauging a prospective business plan or a devious crook who had duped a bevy of investors.

Finally, Harte put down the last piece of paper and leaned back, kneading his eyes with the heels of his palms.

Maddock and Gumby stopped as well, and Maddock rose, saying, "We'd need a whole bucket of bankers to go through this lot to make any sense of it, sir. There's no making head or tail of it as it is. I'm no further along than what we were an hour ago."

As though struck by lightning, Harte sat up straight at his sergeant's words.

"A bucket of bankers! I'm a fool! When I've got the best of the lot sitting in my pocket the whole time! I have to make a call. Keep going through those and see if anything jumps out, but what we need right now is an expert opinion. And I've got just the man for it." So saying, Harte left the room with a skip in his step and went down the stairs two at a time, leaving Maddock and Gumby to look after him in astonishment before exchanging understanding glances and turning back to their work.

"He's got a bee in his bonnet, I'd say. You've got your work cut out for you keeping up with the likes of him! I don't say Maitland doesn't have his points, but it's something to be working with a man that's nimble!"

Maddock could only shake his head as he picked up another closely typed sheet of paper and started reading through it, wondering what his superior could be up to.

Harte, meanwhile, had rushed straight to the telephone and was waiting for a call to go through to Little Bixby.

"Brumble—put his lordship on, will you, it's Harte."

Accustomed to Harte's informal ways, Brumble took no butlerly offense at this cavalier manner and merely went off to inform Lord Fotheringay that his brother-in-law was on the line.

"Rex, a man's got a right to a peaceful evening at home! Lily's already not too happy that you took off at a trot, and now you're butting into a most jolly dinner party, you know."

"I know, and you can tell Lily I'm the worst sort of brother there is, but listen, what do you know about Lord Bartholomew Hemming? Biff Hemming?"

"Why're you nosing around the poor chap? Don't tell me he's finally had enough and offed himself?"

"Offed himself? That bad, was it?"

"No harm in him, poor fellow, but he's never been known for his business smarts, you know. Thought he had his family—or rather, his wife's family—to fall back on though."

"So he did, and he might even come into rather a lot of money. Someone's gone and knocked off his father-in-law. Reginald Timberly. That's why I had to leave in such a hurry. The fellow went and got himself killed during a family party."

"Don't tell me you think old Biff had anything to do with it?"

"He's one of my prime suspects at the moment, in fact. I've just been wading through years and years of shady deals and rotten investments trying to find out if Lord Hemming's the one who made them rotten or if he was just being taken for a ride. Thought I'd put it to you, since you've got your finger on the pulse of anything financial even if you do act the fool most times."

"I'll thank you to know that I act the fool all the time, my good fellow, and don't you tell anyone I'm not one. Comes in handy to be thought a blithering idiot, I've found. People say the damnedest things when they think you can't make head or tail of it."

"Alright, so I'll tell everyone I meet you're just as much of an ass as you come off, will that do? Now do stop chatting away and tell me if I've got a potential swindler and murderer on my hands or if I've just come across the world's biggest dupe."

"Quite the latter, I'm afraid. Apart from the fact that I rather happen to like the chap, and I can't see him stabbing or strangling or whatever it is these murderous fellows do, he's just unfortunately inclined to believe people, no matter what kind of rotters they are."

"Even Mullaney?"

"Don't tell me he was involved with Mullaney? Poor chap! Of course he would be, just the sort of nutter who'd get taken in by Mullaney's charming line."

"What about Farnley? From the papers I've got it looks like old Biff's the one who was doing most of the pulling wool over people's eyes bit."

"Don't talk to me about Farnley. A worse piece of rubbish I've never seen. And he probably got old Biff to believe everything so he'd be all the more convincing when he got others to invest their money. No, old chap, I think you've got the wrong end of the stick if you're trying to pin it on Biff. If I've ever come across anyone who's the perfect mark for a swindler, it's him. In fact, it's a wonder he's relatively unscathed. Some of the fellows he's gone into business with would've had him behind bars if he didn't have that sharp headed father-in-law of his to pull him out when things got too sticky."

"Did he know Timberly was the one to help him out of his messes?"

"I can only assume so. He's always had his wife's family to fall back on, and seems like Timberly—nasty chap, that—was the only one who could've helped him, isn't it?"

Harte sighed and said, "Well, thanks, Fred. I've still got to set my sights on him because he's quite ideally placed to be the murderer, but I'll keep in mind everything you've said."

"Just so, old chap. Onwards and upwards as they say! Chin up! Jolly-o!..."

Smiling despite himself, Harte replaced the telephone and cut off his brother-in-law in mid-sentence. The blithering idiot act was back on, and Harte, for one, wasn't in the mood for it. He turned around to the stairs once again and climbed up slowly, a frown gathering on his brow as he tried to parse out what Fred, a brilliant banker and investor despite all appearances to the contrary, had told him. He smacked the ancient wooden banister with an exasperated sigh and turned to his rooms, where Maddock and Gumby awaited him with more papers and more notes to go through.

## STRIKE TWO

The next morning, Detective Inspector Harte embarked upon his second cup of tea as he tried to find a clue in the photographs that had been delivered early in the morning. His eyes darted from the contorted figure on the bed to the shards of glass, the broken lamp, and the twisted sheets, but nothing jumped out at him.

The inspector had stayed up until the wee hours of the morning going over Maddock's notes and puzzling over the papers Gumby had brought, but the case seemed to elude his grasp every time he came close to making a conclusion. As it was, with what he had to go on, he was hard pressed to choose between Mr. Garth Ashford, Mr. Arthur Pendleton, and Lord Bartholomew Hemming. Although his brother-in-law's words buzzed in Harte's mind, he couldn't quite dismiss Lord Hemming. Each had a motive—primarily money, with the additional motives of avuncular affection for Lord Hemming and a possible un-avuncular affection for Mr. Pendleton. Somehow it didn't seem love or any of the deeper feelings were at play with Mr. Ashford. Each of his suspects had the means—it was highly probable Garth and Arthur had heard where the poison was kept, and Lord Hemming knew, of course. But here the case slipped a bit. Lord Hemming's financial motive dulled a little if what his brother-in-law, Fred, had said was correct, that Lord Timberly had been the one to save Hemming from creditors and swindlers on more than one occasion. What's more, Hemming had no opportunity to enter the conservatory by himself to extract the poison—but he was seen, according to the list Maude and

Lucy had prepared, near Reginald's room holding a tumbler. But what if Hemming wanted to get all of Reginald's money once and for all, instead of having to beg his father-in-law to swoop in and save the day each time?

Harte set him aside and started thinking of the painter again. Garth had entered the conservatory with plenty of opportunity to extract the poison, but the chances of his seeing Reginald in his chambers at night were slim to none. Had he, however, finagled his way in to see Reginald? Possible, Harte mused, but unlikely. Arthur, of course, had had Fernet with his godfather—the ideal time to slip him some poison. But he had only entered the conservatory after this perfect opportunity. Harte kept staring at Maude and Lucy's list, trying to grasp the clue he instinctively felt was hidden in plain sight there, but that refused to materialize for him. With the information at hand and with his brother-in-law's words about Lord Hemming's lack of financial prowess, it appeared Garth was his best suspect so far. However, a persnickety sense of justice kept Harte from jumping to a conclusion that would nicely wrap the case up in a bow, but would be based on the most circumstantial of evidence and a few too many ifs.

"Excuse me, Detective Inspector Harte, I presume?"

Harte looked up, instantly shuffling the photographs into their envelope, and saw a short, tubby little man, his narrow nose adorned with old-fashioned, gold rimmed pince nez, his bald pate unconvincingly covered with long grey strands of hair combed over from his right ear to his left, and shaggy eyebrows above eyes an indiscriminate shade of rheumy brown. A double chin moved slightly over a precise grey bow tie, and the matching suit was impeccably tailored. Holding out a soft, pale hand, the voice that had not yet lost its sharp, steely edge despite the years uttered, "I am Nugent Jellaby. I believe we have an appointment. I was Lord Reginald Timberly's solicitor and am the executor of his will."

In response to Harte's smile and acknowledgment of this introduction, Sir Nugent Jellaby lowered his portly form with some difficulty into the narrow chair across from Harte's and deposited a well-worn briefcase at his side.

When the lawyer had been provided with a cup of tea, Harte jumped into his questions. "A pleasure to meet you, sir. And thank you for stopping in to see me before you go to Timberly. I just wanted to get the lay of the land, as it were, from you. Was there anything Lord Timberly wanted to see you about in particular? I learned he had especially asked you to visit, presumably to change his will. Had he mentioned any specific changes?"

"A sad business, a very sad business." Jellaby's second chin quivered for an instant. Mid-quiver, the muddy brown eyes popped open with a shrewd look. "Lord Reginald Timberly was prone to changing his will at—er—will." Allowing himself a little smile at this sally, the lawyer continued. "But these changes were typically only cosmetic. I think he rather enjoyed 'changing his will' to see how many hoops his heirs would jump through at the threat. Of course, he had, on occasion, written out his children or other heirs. Although he changed his will quite often, when he made the decision to cut out any of his direct heirs, this decision was not taken lightly. When he chose to disinherit his daughter— Miss Julie Bosworth's mother and Lady Hemming's sister— he did not again even mention the possibility of including her in his will. When I last spoke with him, he did say he wanted to change his will so the money would be tied up dependent on Miss Julie's marriage to Mr. Pendleton. In fact, one of my goals in visiting him was to persuade him to change his mind—in so far as he would take my counsel, of course. He had not mentioned anything about Lady Hemming, and I was not under the impression that he meant to change any provisions in her regard. He also wished to see me as he saw some changes in property leases coming up. I have the papers with me, if you would like to see them."

"Thank you, I should. I believe the case is tied up with this changing of the will business, but it would be prudent to see what else Lord Timberly had on his mind."

"If you don't mind my asking—are there any—er—what I mean to say is, do you suppose I shall be called upon to assist Lord and Lady Hemming or Miss Bosworth? I am by way of being the solicitor for the Pendletons as well. Close families, the two of them, although of course now there aren't many left of either the Timberlys or the Pendletons."

"I can't say as yet. I certainly hope not, for their sakes. And I see it falls to me to inform you. It seems Miss Bosworth is, in fact, Mrs. Garth Ashford, and has been for at least a few weeks."

A frown creasing his face and his chin wobbling dangerously, Sir Jellaby said, "How is this? I have not heard anything of the matter. It is most irregular. Are you quite certain—" Jellaby directed one discerning look at Harte's face, "—but of course you are sure. As I said, a very sad business. I assume this young man has little to recommend him? It was always Lord Timberly's conviction Miss—er—his granddaughter would fall prey to a money hunter."

"I'm afraid—it appears the marriage has not lived up to Mrs. Ashford's expectations. She was most distraught when she revealed the secret last night. In fact, it appears Mr. Ashford has been behaving rather—ignobly, shall we say—since it had become clear Lord Timberly was about to change his will unfavorably for himself."

Raising his eyebrows slowly, Nugent Jellaby shot a clear look at Harte. "Oh-ho. It's like that, is it?" Straightening his back a little, he said somberly, "If it should be Julie's wish, I shall, of course, have to make my services available to her husband. I have been in this business too long not to know which way the wind is blowing, and I can only say I hope there was no means or opportunity for Mr.—Ash—Ashford, is it?—to have been involved in this farce. As to the motive, I fear we need not look too far."

Bowing a little, Harte said, "I'm afraid so, and I see we understand each other. I have no wish to keep you longer, but if you care to wait for a few moments, I am about to head up to the house. May I offer you a ride? My sergeant should be along any minute—"

And indeed, just at that moment, Sergeant Maddock tumbled into the inn's parlor, eyes almost falling out of his head. He came to a rather abrupt halt upon seeing his superior seated with an elderly man whose snapping eyes betrayed his curiosity although his demeanor did not otherwise show any spirit of inquiry at all.

Slowing his steps to a more sedate pace, Sergeant Maddock approached the table. "Could I have a moment, sir? I'm afraid there's a development that requires your attention."

Harte, looking up at his Sergeant and, noting the perspiring nose, the red tinted cheeks and the fact that he appeared even more hake-like than usual, stood up and bowed politely to Sir Jellaby, excusing himself.

Harte closed the parlor door behind him, walked a little way down the hall where there was nobody else present and snapped, "Well, man, get on with it. Although for all you've managed to keep it under your hat, you may as well have spilled the beans right then and there in front of Sir Jellaby— that's the solicitor we've been waiting for, by the way. Out with it! If you've come to tell me either Ashford or Pendleton has absconded and left behind a confession, I'll be glad of it!"

Wiping his brow, his sergeant said slowly, "If it were only that, sir, I'd be smiling and whistling it to the world. As it is...I'm afraid, sir, there's been another death. Another murder!"

"What!" At this, Harte's head shot up in earnest and his eyes started glinting dangerously. A grim frown settled on his face.

"Yes, sir. A call just came through for you to the inn, and I took it as I was on the spot. They thought it best to call us in first, since we're already involved. Mr. Garth Ashford was found in the library this morning by the maid who went in to clean out the fireplace. A nasty shock for her, sir, by all accounts."

"Any chance of accident at all?" Harte's brain was working furiously, and he was already walking back toward the parlor, quickly re-assessing Ashford's role in the murder of Reginald Timberly.

"No, sir. His head's been bashed in."

Entering the parlor, Harte approached Sir Jellaby, still sitting in his chair as they had left him.

"I'm afraid, sir, I'll have to go up to the house immediately." Turning to his sergeant, Harte spoke in a clipped voice. "Get the local fingerprints men, medical man, the usual. Bring the car around, we'll be off right away." Maddock nodded and went off and Harte turned back to Sir Jellaby. "You're welcome to join, if you wish, but I must warn you it's likely to be rather unpleasant. There's been another death—another murder, in fact. Mr. Garth Ashford."

The look on Sir Nugent Jellaby's face would have made the inspector laugh out loud at any other time. The typically disinterested mouth went slack, the rheumy eyes seemed to grow three sizes, and the finicky gold pince nez were in danger of slipping right off his nose. Recovering himself somewhat, and seeming to realize his duty, the lawyer straightened and put his hands, shaking slightly, up to his bow tie, adjusting it infinitesimally. "Yes. Yes, I believe I shall be needed." Wagging his head gravely to himself, he said again as he picked up his briefcase, "A sad case. And I see I shall undoubtedly be needed."

Harte had already turned on his heel and was striding toward the door. It was only when he had his hand on the door knob that he paused. He turned his head to give Jellaby a straight gaze and said in the same clipped voice, "I'm afraid so, sir. As you are the solicitor for the Pendletons as well as Lord Timberly's family, it seems inevitable."

*

At Timberly, the house was in chaos. Jennie, the maid who had discovered the body, had only waited until she reached the domains of the kitchen and announced her exciting news before promptly collapsing into a nervous faint. Jennings took off at what could only be described as a trot, dragging one of the footmen with him. Cook started having palpitations and announced she was no use to anyone and had never been one to stand up to shock. Another maid, perhaps a little disappointed it had not been she who discovered the ugly sight of a man with his head pounded in, said she felt ever so queasy and had to be supported to a chair next to Cook, both seeking to comfort themselves and each other by declaring loud and long that they didn't know what to do and what the world was coming to. The gardener's boy, who had the good fortune of being present in the kitchen to drop off some vegetables, added his two cents, declaring the house was sure to be haunted now that two murderous deaths had occurred within twenty-four hours of each other. The fulfillment of these precise conditions for ghosts to occur set off palpitations even in those present who had not yet succumbed to their heretofore latent sensitivities.

Jennie awoke from her faint to find her position as chief witness usurped by a number of relatively unimportant personages whose protestations of distress were quickly making them the center of attention. It was only Mrs. Basset's firm handling that managed to subdue the rising hue and cry brought on by Jennie's announcement, and it was several minutes until the kitchen had returned to some semblance of calm. Only a few sobs and hiccups sounded from time to time, and although Cook had announced her palpitations meant she couldn't prepare lunch (or any other meals for the foreseeable future, for that matter) and had been presented with a cup of tea, the rest of the staff were ready to return to their tasks.

As it was an awkward time when the household was coming downstairs to breakfast and the servants were waiting to clean the rooms, none of the maids had the opportunity to spread the news as they would no doubt have wished. Indeed, it was only Jennings' failure to appear in the breakfast room that raised any questions at all. The house party had risen betimes and were seating themselves at the breakfast table or helping themselves to kedgeree and sausages, when Jennings entered. Lucy, glancing up as he opened the door, was immediately struck by his pallor, and watched with interest as he made his way over to Biff and bent to whisper something in his ear.

He may as well have shouted his message to the whole room, for the effect on his employer was electrifying. Biff jumped out of his seat as if he had been shot and gawped, "Ashford's dead?!"

The effect on the rest of the table was no less animating. Maude dropped the spoon of marmalade on the pristine white tablecloth at the precise moment Marty let go of the serving spoon for the eggs, splattering scrambled eggs around the buffet. Julie half-rose out of the chair but uttered nothing but a gasp and, turning a sickly white, sat down again with an indelicate thump. Arthur went to her, laying a hand on her shoulder and nodding as she raised large, tearful eyes to him. She grasped his hand as though it were a lifeline. Harris rose, set down his knife and fork, just loaded with a portion of sausage, and went toward Jennings, saying urgently, "What is this, man? Ashford killed? I'll go to the library at once!" and took off.

Only Lucy, who had seen Jennings' face and had a moment to prepare herself for some bad news, had not dropped or spilled anything. She had observed, instead, everyone else's reactions. She walked over to Marty and reached out to clasp her hand. Her friend was still a little stiff over their disclosures to Detective Inspector Harte, but she took Lucy's hand with relief. After a moment, Lucy made her way over to Biff, who seemed to have recovered himself and was hearing from Jennings that the body was in the library and should they call in the local constabulary.

"Call the inn instead, Jennings. Biff, Inspector Harte is staying there. I'm sure he'll get the local men as well, but he'll have to know first, I think."

"Yes, yes of course. An excellent idea. Call Inspector Harte, Jennings. And close up the library of course. He'll want to make sure nothing's touched. Oh—of course, Dr. Witting's gone to make sure—but—but there's no doubt, is there?"

On his last few words, Harris entered again, saying somberly, "I'm afraid there's nothing to be done. I've locked the door. Here's the key," and handed it to Biff. Lucy, catching sight of his face, wondered if she had ever seen the young doctor looking more stone-like than this.

When Jennings had departed, Biff turned back to the table, looking dumbstruck. It was Arthur who broke the silence. Not, as Lucy half-expected, to make some jest about returning to their meal, but to ask Maude, seated next to Julie, to take the stricken girl up to her room. Julie was looking as though she might keel over at any moment. She clung to Arthur's hand as he supported her to the door, and turned big, pleading eyes to him. "It—it wasn't—" Arthur said in a curiously gentle voice, "No, of course not. Go upstairs, I'm sure it will be alright." And turning to give a tight smile to Maude, he stepped away from Julie. Maude took Julie's arm and turned briefly to cast a searching look at Lucy. The placid face gave away nothing to anyone else but told her best friend volumes. Swallowing once, Maude turned back to Julie and helped her make her way up the stairs as though she was in a trance.

When the two had departed, everyone else sat down again. The eggs congealed in front of them and nobody broke the silence until Jennings arrived, once again, to announce the arrival of Detective Inspector Harte, Sergeant Maddock, and Sir Nugent Jellaby.

# RETURN TO QUERIES

Harte stood with his arms crossed, his eyebrows lowered, looking down at the body slumped over the arm of a leather wing back chair by the fire. The basket of brushes and papers the maid would have used to clean out the fireplace lay discarded by the cold fireplace, the ash ground into the fine Turkish carpet. A small part of Harte's brain wondered disinterestedly whether they would ever be able to get the thick black marks out. He had been present in Little Bixby on one occasion when his sister's children had played trains with a full ashtray to serve as their overly realistic steam cloud, and could still remember the spate of scrubbing and cleaning Lily's housekeeper had had to undertake. Another part of his brain was focused on the other stains on the carpet, where the blood that had dripped from Garth Ashford's head to the floor now lay dull and congealed. A brass and mahogany bar cart stood just behind the chair, grotesque in its appearance of normalcy. A matching leather wingback chair, a pair to the one occupied by the body, was also pulled up to the fire as though for an intimate chat. What had Garth been talking about, and with whom? What conversation could lead to such a deadly end?

"I suppose the poor sod didn't bash his own head in and then hide the weapon, did he sir? There goes our prime suspect."

Harte continued staring at the body, the marks on the carpet, the ash, the bar cart, the fire irons, the chairs.

"Didn't see it coming, did he, sir?" repeated Sergeant Maddock.

Looking up at Maddock, Harte replied, "No. I shouldn't think he did. He wouldn't have sat there calmly while someone he feared came up behind him. But..." Surveying the scene, Harte fell silent again. After a few moments, he spoke, still in that grim tone. "Where's the weapon, Maddock? Where's the weapon? As you said, our prime suspect wouldn't have conveniently offed himself and hidden the weapon to boot. And anyway, banging yourself over the head isn't the most conventional way a murderer confesses and commits suicide. Those fire irons will have to be gone over, but I can't quite see a chap just sitting there as his conversation companion rises, takes up a fire poker and walks around this table and the bar cart, up behind his chair, do you? Get the fingerprints men to go over the whole fireplace carefully. And the bar cart too—every bottle, every glass. Every inch of this room. Although the whole lot of them have been in and out of here for the past few days, so I'm sure all it'll turn up is a mess of fingerprints and no clues whatsoever. And the medical man will be able to tell us if it was a fire iron or something else. We'll have to get on to Dr. Witting too, to see what he thought of it. Came in to ascertain the death, didn't he? Although if the maid couldn't tell the man was dead, she'd have to be a Bedlamite."

Maddock nodded and wondered if the murderer was running scared. As he watched Harte going over the scene, he thought now that the killer had done it again, it was only a matter of time before the noose tightened. No amateur could get away with two murders one after the other in a closed setting like this.

As if reading his mind, Harte said slowly, "And so...we have it. The tangle is thicker than ever, Maddock, thicker than ever. We'll go into this murder, of course, but we need to look over those statements again. We've got something there, otherwise the murderer wouldn't have taken such a drastic action. Ashford must have known something. All we've got to do is to recognize it. It's always when the knot seems undoable that something slips, and we'll get him."

"Or her, sir."

Shooting a grim look at his sergeant, Harte repeated, "Or her."

\*

Detective Inspector Harte sat across the table from Garth Ashford's widow, taking in the shaking hands, the red rimmed eyes, the shiny nose, and, most of all, the fear stricken eyes. For Julie was afraid, terrified even. But was it fear of being caught or fear for someone else? So far Harte had not been able to find the answer. He had received only the briefest of responses, which led him to understand Garth had not said anything at dinner, had not appeared in any way different, had not mentioned meeting anyone or wanting to speak with anyone in particular, and had stayed downstairs after everyone had retired to bed. These singularly unhelpful statements were only gleaned after a series of confusing—purposefully so, Harte thought—retractions and revisions, until it was a miracle Sergeant Maddock's pencil had not gone right through his paper with frustration. They were seated in the drawing room as the library was still occupied by the fingerprints men and the local medical man, and Harte had felt it imprudent to question the dead man's widow in the same room as the body. Maddock, seated slightly behind Julie, did not envy Harte. Questioning a frightened young woman was never an easy task, and especially if the damsel in question might have been the very person who had murdered her husband in cold blood.

At the end of a fruitless hour, Harte leaned forward, clasping his hands in front of him. "I want to help you. You don't need to be afraid. We aren't monsters, and we're rather enamored of the truth. You needn't be afraid I'll arrest—anyone—on mere suspicion or the presence of a motive. It will be hard fact, and fact only, that will have any bearing on the case." Seeing no response other than Julie's refusal to meet his gaze, he sighed and said in a gentle tone, "I see how it is. I hope you will keep my words in mind. I only wish to assist you in finding your husband's murderer. If you think of anything that would be at all helpful—or unhelpful—please, come talk to me." He rose and escorted her out of the drawing room wondering if the previous hour had been a complete waste. Had he at least been able to make some slight impression upon the nervous young lady?

"Do you think it's her or that Pendleton chap, sir?" As soon as the door had closed behind Julie, Maddock had risen to stretch his legs and flex his fingers.

"You'll do well to remember not to jump to conclusions, my good fellow! I only wanted to see her first as she's the widow—although whether she's grieving for her husband or for the murderer, I don't yet know. I shouldn't have thought it was the husband, in any event. I think we'll see the maid, then Jennings, and then Witting. They were all first at the scene, weren't they? Let's try and get the thing clear. And perhaps they can tell us what everyone's movements were last night as well."

*

Jennie entered the room holding Mrs. Basset's hand, accompanied by Mr. Jennings for support, and quite obviously apprehensive of getting arrested right then and there. After ten minutes of Harte's cajoling and gentle questioning, Maddock was ready to arrest her after all, if only to stop her from going on as though the inspector were an inquisitor and she an innocent accused of heresy. It was only through the inspector's delicate handling that Jennie calmed down enough to give a half-way coherent account of finding the body. This highly elaborated narrative included such interesting events as "coming over queer" and "swooning away" (she did not actually faint, as Harte ascertained after a few more questions) and boiled down to only about two or three sentences of useful information. Namely, Jennie had entered the library, which had not been locked, and had made her way straight to the fireplace to clean and remake the fire. Because the curtains were drawn, she had spied the body just as she was about to kneel down (hence the spilled cleaning materials and ash ground into the carpet—for which Mrs. Basset directed a dark look at her, raising sympathy in Harte's chest). She had turned tail without touching a thing other than the door, and had run straight to the kitchen to tell her tale.

This Mrs. Basset corroborated, as did the butler. Jennings had been about to go to the breakfast room, where the family and guests would be arriving and where the food had already been set out. In fact, he had only come downstairs to inquire after a special marmalade Lady Hemming preferred but that had not been replenished. He gave the inspector a clear, if halting, account of his own movements. He had run up to the library with one of the footmen, had entered the door left open by Jennie (here he sent a disapproving glare toward the little maid, who instantly took refuge in Mrs. Basset's shoulder), and had gone toward the fireplace. Neither he nor the footman had touched anything. They had come away when it was immediately clear there was nothing to be done for poor Mr. Ashford. Jennings had closed the door behind them when they left the library.

Here he paused to explain to the inspector that he had left the library unlocked the previous night as Mr. Ashford and Mr. Pendleton were still sitting there, having a glass of whiskey, when he did his nightly rounds. He had not thought it right to interrupt, but he assured the inspector there was nothing amiss. Although both gentlemen had drinks in hand, they seemed to be having a fairly amiable, if strained, discussion.

Harte felt it politic not to explore too closely how Mr. Jennings was able to arrive at such a precise judgment of the conversation without listening rather closely, and asked him to continue. The butler only added that after leaving the library this morning, he and the footman had proceeded to the breakfast room, where he had discreetly notified Lord

Hemming of Mr. Ashford's death. Lord Hemming, in turn, had notified the gathered company, shouting out "Ashford's dead?!" Jennings' stiff tone made it clear he did not approve of thus announcing that Mr. Ashford was deceased, but he did think it creditable of the doctor to run off to the library immediately without even pausing to hear the rest of the tale, to see if there was anything to be done. Jennings assured the inspector he had been on the verge of explaining there was indeed nothing to be done, but the doctor had left precipitately.

It had been Miss Belling who suggested calling Inspector Harte in addition to the local constabulary. Dr. Witting had come back to confirm there was nothing more to be done for Mr. Ashford. Miss Maude had escorted Miss Julie—or Mrs. Ashford, as Jennings had only recently learned (the stiff posture said much about the affront Jennings had suffered and his conservative views on the matter) to her room and stayed with her. Everyone else had remained in the breakfast room. Nobody had eaten breakfast.

There seemed to be little more to be gathered from either Jennie, Mrs. Basset or Mr. Jennings, and Harte dismissed them with a sigh. In a weary voice he said, "Dr. Witting, I think, Maddock."

\*

Harris Witting entered with his measured tread, inquiring politely how he could be of assistance.

"Could you tell us what you know about Mr. Ashford's death, Dr. Witting?"

"He appeared to have been hit over the head. I'm sure your man will tell you the details, but it was quite evident he had been killed by a blunt instrument. He must have been dead less than twelve hours when I saw him. Unfortunate, really. I understood he would have made a name for himself in a few years."

"Did you speak with him last night? Were you aware of

any assignations or appointments he had made to meet with anyone last night in the library?"

"I'm afraid we didn't have much conversation. In fact, everyone was subdued, given recent events. After dinner, the ladies retired rather quickly, as did I."

"But you knew Mr. Ashford was in the library?"

"I believe Jennings mentioned something of the sort." Harris paused, appeared to engage in what Harte deemed a very short battle with his scruples, and went on. "I must admit, it also jumped to mind as—as—a likely place for his body to be if he had been murdered. I have no wish to incriminate anyone, Inspector, I hope you understand. But given what has happened I see it is my duty to tell you everything, no matter how trivial it may seem. It's just that I had overheard Garth and Arthur speaking with each other during cocktails, just as dinner was announced. I heard Arthur promising Garth they would finish their conversation later if he would meet him for a drink in the library. Of course, when Jennings said Garth had been killed, that little piece of conversation must have clicked in my mind. When I arrived I saw immediately there was no possibility of helping him. The poor fellow never stood a chance."

"You did not know what they were to speak of?"

"No, but of course," again, Harris paused briefly before continuing, "I have, for some time, thought there was something of an understanding between Julie and Arthur. I should hate to suggest...but then, you will no doubt find the answer yourself. It just seemed to me a little odd that Arthur pretends to have cared little for his godfather's money when it isn't really clear at all what his own means are. Also funny that he pretends to be disinterested in the woman he's been dangling after for as long as memory serves. She, too, seemed to have been disillusioned about her—late—husband in the previous day or two. I did wonder. But again, I am not given to speculation."

"Thank you, Dr. Witting. If there's nothing else, I think that will be all."

The door closed behind the doctor, and Harte and Maddock exchanged a grave look.

"Darker and darker for Mr. Pendleton, sir. Not that I'm finding the doctor any more charming, but there it is."

"Yes. Yes, it would appear so. Let's take another look at your notes, Sergeant. If I am not mistaken—and I am rarely mistaken—there is something there we have missed. No doubt you took down a whole lot of rubbish to obscure the real clues, but there, I'll let it go this time."

Nodding genially, Sergeant Maddock agreed. "Ay, and it's me who has the motive to go hiding all the good clues, sir. Like to see you wade through a case with only half the information, you know. See if what the boys at the Yard say about you being a sharp 'un is actually true!"

Their eyes meeting in grim humor, the two men sighed and started shuffling through the morass of notes once again.

## REVELATIONS FOR THE RECORD

At lunch, the party was sadly reduced and extremely subdued. Marty, still a little stiff with Maude and Lucy even though suspicion now appeared to have veered from herself and Biff to Arthur, was eating lunch on a tray upstairs with Julie. This young lady, especially when she heard Arthur was to speak with the inspector next, had rushed upstairs to her room and holed up again. Arthur himself was still in the drawing room with the Scotland Yard men. Biff was in a brown study, muttering to himself from time to time that it couldn't be, it just couldn't be, and he couldn't make out who had done it. Although he didn't seem to blame Lucy and Maude for having pointed the hounds in his direction, he appeared too preoccupied to be much of a host. Feeling it best to make themselves scarce, Lucy, giving Maude a slight nod, rose and excused herself. Maude followed her into the hall, exclaiming, "Well that's shot up the whole place!"

"Ssh! Not here. Come out onto the terrace with me, will you?"

Settling themselves on a bench by a rose bush, the two turned to each other.

"Maudie, things are bad."

"It looks like they suspect Arthur, doesn't it? I don't know, Luce, it doesn't seem right somehow. Not that I can imagine any of the rest of us doing something horrid like that, but bashing in Garth's head...it almost doesn't seem like Arthur *in particular*, does it? I mean to say—I can see him poisoning someone, horrible as it is to imagine, but this kind of violence—somehow it doesn't fit."

"You're right, Maude. I've been going over it time after time. And somehow I keep running up against the fact that this was such a—such a *crude* murder. The poison at least seemed to have some delicacy to it, didn't it? But this was just outright violence. Somehow I can't see Arthur picking up a fire iron or something."

Maude gave Lucy a sideways glance and said, "Although I'm sure, if what I think is true, he's glad to see someone's brained Garth. Do you think Julie loves Arthur too, Lucy?"

Not the least startled by this jump, Lucy raised serious eyes to her friend's face. "You don't think—he wouldn't! Julie could easily have divorced Garth—perhaps even annulled it. There was no reason to take such drastic action, surely? Unless maybe he wouldn't give her a divorce."

"And there would be the scandal, of course."

"No, the scandal wouldn't do it. There's the rub, Maude. If they do actually love each other, Julie and Arthur have motives to kill Garth, but why do it when a less nasty solution exists? If it's true Garth was after Julie for the money, I'm sure he could have been bought off, paid off, something, to assure a divorce. But would Arthur or Julie choose to kill the man instead and risk everything? It doesn't fit! And that's assuming the two love each other, when we don't know anything of the sort."

Shaking her head, Maude rose and went over to the steps leading down into the garden. There was a dark mist curling around the grounds, somehow heavier and more depressing than the roiling fury of the thunderstorms of the past couple of days. "I know Marty and Biff are going almost mad with this—this horror. I thought when we made that silly little list we were helping somehow. But now, I feel like—oh if only there were something we could do! I know Rex and his sergeant won't do anything rash, but I do feel like we should have heard something or seen something that would have helped, don't you?"

"You know, maybe you're right. But I don't know what. What was Garth talking about yesterday? Was there anything that would have set off—well—anyone, really?" Lucy couldn't quite help the images of her friends flashing past her mind, but she refused to say their names out loud as suspects.

Maude turned to her and said eagerly, "Yes! There must be! What did he say? When we all found out Julie and he were married—he seemed—well I don't know, put off? And remember how oily he was about the whole marriage thing—trying to tell Julie she'd trapped him? Oh! But I'm just making a case for why Garth must have killed Reginald, when we're now trying to find out who killed Garth!"

"Do you know, I somehow don't think, now, that it was Garth who had anything to do with Reginald's murder. He seemed to be quite alright in the morning, before Julie let the cat out of the bag, didn't he? Kept going on about some old lady. Who was it? I don't know, but do you remember, at lunch he was gossiping on about something or the other. And afterwards, he became a little too smooth, a little too gracious, and making too many excuses for not telling us they were married. But I suppose he didn't know Julie had let that bit slip about him saying she'd trapped him. Ugh! I'm going all around in circles. Do you think the library's been cleared out, Maude?"

"You don't want to go poking about his—his body, do you?!" Maude exclaimed, nauseated, but with a gleam of curiosity at the prospect. "Do you suppose they'd let us? We'd have to wear a mask or something at the very least!"

"No, silly! You are the utter limit! As if they'd let the two of us go poking about a crime scene! Not that I'd want to see a dead—murdered—body anyway, with his—its—head bashed in." Lucy gave a shudder, out of place with her usual practical demeanor. "But what I really wanted to do is to clear our heads a bit. Mind helping me go through some old newspapers and finding some interesting stories for my next writing project? I'm a bit stuck with my heroine right now, and I could use a few juicy, gossipy little tidbits for inspiration. Maybe base the next episode in the Hon. Holly Galbraith's life on something from the papers."

Maude, giving her own delicate shudder in response, said, "And I'm the limit? Although I suppose if we want some peace and quiet, and if you want to clear your head, the library would be the place for it. I don't think any of the others will come within a mile of it! And not that I'm too keen either, but let's go see if it's open to use. I suppose I'll just have to overcome my maidenly scruples and help you go through those musty newspapers. I think Biff keeps all of his for the last year or two, doesn't he? I must say, he would be ever so much happier if he and Marty could just inherit Reginald's money and he could settle down to cataloguing his library and poring over his orchids while Marty drifts around and has tea with us."

So saying, the two friends slipped off the terrace and off to the library to go over "musty newspapers."

*

In the drawing room, Arthur Pendleton was finding it hard going with a steely-eyed inspector and a sergeant who, Arthur was sure, kept sending scorching looks toward his back. His smooth appearance was a little shaken and his eyes showed the strain. His collar was limp, he kept tugging at his cuffs, and even his shoes seemed to have lost some of their luster.

"I don't quite know what you want me to say. Yes, I had a drink with Garth. No, I did not brain him with a poker or whatever else I'm supposed to have used. He was hale and hearty when I left him, just as Uncle Reg was hale and hearty when I left him after having a glass of Fernet with him. If you still suspect me of Reginald's murder, check with my bank if you want. I had no need of his money then, nor do I now."

It had taken an hour to even reach this begrudging permission, but Harte nodded to Maddock. Pendleton's finances would have to be gone into carefully. However, it was troubling that he seemed ready to share this information voluntarily. It appeared his earlier refusal was merely his desire to be troublesome and uncooperative, but if he truly did not lack for money it destroyed the motive in the first murder at least. Grasping at straws, Harte wondered if perhaps Arthur's money came from shady deals. Did Arthur only appear solvent at his bank, but have debts that would have to be paid off?

"If you must know, I was talking to him about Julie. Of course she doesn't know it—she and I haven't talked about it at all. But Garth got the idea that I'd be happy to buy him off for a divorce."

They were back to one of the main lines of Arthur's testimony. He seemed bent on proving Julie had no reason to harm Garth, nor could she have done it. Harte wondered why Arthur cared so much whether Julie had a motive or not. He knew there had once been something between them, but was it just leftover affection or something more? It was fairly evident Julie was still in love with Arthur. The man seated across from him, however, was a cool customer, and Harte couldn't quite make out what his intentions were. Were Julie and Arthur accomplices? Was Arthur still in love with Julie and had he killed Garth to get him out of the way? But then again, if they had been discussing a divorce...There were just too many ifs. The only fact he had was that Arthur Pendleton seemed to be the last man to have seen Garth Ashford alive. And the last man to have seen the dead fellow alive was, in nine cases out of ten, the murderer himself. Harte gave himself a mental shake and brought his mind back to the questions at hand.

"You may very well give me permission to look into your bank records, but I must know how you come by your money. You must see, if it is money easily won and easily lost through debts for instance, I must know that. And I must know on what basis you believed you could buy Garth Ashford off and prompt him to give his wife a divorce. And why Mrs. Ashford should be amenable to it." Noticing Arthur's face stiffen, Harte decided to make a risky move. "In fact, sir, I must tell you that at the moment we can't help but look with suspicion upon Mrs. Ashford. She was a little too quick to defend you about her grandfather's murder. She was unhappy in her marriage to Mr. Ashford. She would have raised no fears in Mr. Ashford's mind if she were to approach him from the back with some sort of heavy implement. He may have been wary of a man who had just been asking him to divorce his wife, but he would not be so wary of his own wife. Mrs. Ashford stands to gain a lot from the removal of Mr. Garth Ashford."

At this Arthur's hands shot up into his hair, disheveling his carefully ordered locks into a bird's nest. His face set, he laughed grimly and said, "Quite the wrong end of the stick there, my good fellow. I know Ashford would've divorced Julie only because he told me so, as I've just been telling you. You policemen aren't much for paying attention are you? And Julie is an old friend who's about to get something pinned on her when it shouldn't be. What difference does it make to you how I make my money? How will it affect Julie anyway? I own a damned lingerie business, damn you. Go ask around about Madame Sardon's lingerie and you'll see it in every elite boutique in the country! I would go to any length to hide the fact that this whole gentleman of leisure aura I cultivate is funded by a highly profitable women's lingerie business, but there it is! If it will convince you Julie didn't do it! She knows about the whole business and about how much money I have. And she knows I cared for my godfather. That's why she would never suspect me of killing Reginald! And if you've been taken in by that languid attitude she affects, then I can only say, more fool you! The little wretch—she couldn't even lift a finger to harm an ant, much less that slimy bounder who tricked her into marrying him!"

Trying hard to keep his face straight in the face of this astounding revelation, Harte quickly and studiously avoided catching Maddock's gaze. He knew his sergeant would be giving him the look peculiar to a highly excited fish, and his mustache would be quivering in delight. Harte looked down at his hands to hide from Arthur the involuntary smile that crossed his face. To think of the sleek, urbane Mr. Pendleton, making his money as a producer and seller of women's lingerie! But, and Harte became grave again, a woman who knew this ridiculous fact and still loved him—what would she do to escape her sham of a marriage and be able to marry a rich, self-sustaining man who loved her too?

"Then I must ask you once again, sir, was there anything at all you noticed when you left Mr. Ashford? Was there any reason he stayed behind instead of going upstairs with you when you had finished your drink?"

"I keep telling you, he seemed to be waiting for someone—not Julie, because he specifically said he would talk to her tomorrow—today—the next day. He was quite taken with this idea of me financing their divorce, although I can't tell why he should've got that particular bee in his bonnet. I think he had some idea of approaching Julie about it the next day. At the risk of sounding like a cad, I should say it's fairly evident how she feels about me. But he did seem to be waiting for someone. I don't know who it could be. When I was going upstairs I asked him if he was coming too, but he only poured himself another measure of Uncle Reg's twenty year Scotch—poor old fellow would have been enraged to see it go down that bounder's gullet—and set it down on the little table between us, saying he had other things to attend to. It definitely seemed as though he was waiting for someone. But I can't say he was excited or—or—apprehensive or anything of the sort. In fact, he didn't really seem to have any idea what was coming, if I could speculate a little." With an effort at regaining his smooth manner, Arthur went on. "Certainly not for a woman. He didn't seem eager, but just a little curious, perhaps a little bored."

"I see. Thank you, sir, that will be all." Seeing the wary look Arthur directed at him, Harte was moved to say, "We rarely catch the wrong man—or woman—you know. But let me know if you think of anything else that might be helpful."

When Arthur had left, the two Scotland Yard men faced each other to compare notes. Neither knew exactly what to make of Pendleton. It seemed evident he was trying to protect Julie, but both Harte and Maddock were doubtful about why. Could it just be platonic affection? Or was it something deeper? Arthur had certainly protested that he had not broached the topic of divorce, but that was an easy enough lie to come up with to hide a murder. On one point, however, Harte was inclined to believe Pendleton. Was Garth Ashford really waiting up for somebody? And if it wasn't anything he was excited or apprehensive about, who could it be?

"Find out from the fingerprints men whether that bar cart had a bottle of twenty year old Scotch on it, will you? Let's see who else handled it. It should have Mr. Ashford's prints on it clear as the day, but perhaps it'll give us a clue about who else might have had a drink with him too."

Maddock nodded, and rose to go to the telephone, saying, "He's a cool one, sir. I don't quite trust him, and he's a sight too ready to stick up for that Miss Julie. But from what Miss Julie's maid said about her going to bed early and taking some sleeping powders, I should say it wasn't her as done him in. You said the more tangled it gets the sooner it slips, but I'm not seeing any loose threads for us to pull on just yet, sir. Perhaps this here bottle will give us something to chew on finally."

# GOSSIP IN THE LIBRARY

"Ooh here's something, Luce! Any interest in a bride who ran away two days before the marriage, came back and married the groom's best friend at the wedding that had already been planned?"

"Oof! A little too awkward, don't you think? And quite involved too! Besides, Holly Galbraith already has two love interests, and I don't want her married off just yet. It's a series after all. I don't think my publisher will be too happy if I don't keep the saga going a little longer! I was thinking maybe something a little darker, more real, you know? Perhaps a death or something." Seeing Maude's expression, Lucy smiled and shook her head. "Got it on the brain I guess! But I think if I write it out maybe it'll help, don't you?"

The two continued flipping through the newspapers exclaiming here and there.

"Oh look, Maude. Here's an article—no, obituary—on that Mrs. Garfield from Chilton who used to breed pugs. I didn't know she left Harris a lot of money when she died. In fact, I didn't even know she was his patient. Wasn't that the woman Garth was talking about? Maybe he'd been talking about it with Harris?"

"Yes, I think she left him quite a lot, actually. When I had tea with his mother—ghastly woman, utterly too clingy—she said it actually got Harris out of a rough spot. I think it was just around a time he desperately needed money. The practice wasn't doing so well or something. But Mrs. Witting—I'm sure she meant to show me just what a wonderful husband Harris would make—said how Harris's patients truly loved him, and he'd been remembered in a legacy or two that helped set him not just right, but quite prosperously so. Kind of horrid to be glad someone popped off just in time to save you from the River Tick, I say."

"Lucky for him, I suppose. I wonder if there's something in here about the other woman too—do you remember her name?"

"Harth? Hatting? Hattison? Hatton?"

Lucy started laughing. "Stop! Stop! I don't think I can stand your recitations of all the surnames you can think of starting with an H! Let's just keep looking, shall we? I'm sure it'll be in the obituaries if you think it's around the same time. I wonder if I can make the Hon. Holly have a great aunt or something who dies? Maybe she could leave her some money or a house or something. Give her a project—maybe something like what I'm doing with the old manse."

About ten minutes later, Maude looked up, saying, "I think I've got her! Mrs. Nancy Hattison. Left a few legacies here and there. Nothing much else, really, except she's survived by one son."

A tap sounded and Mrs. Basset opened the door to the library, poking her head around the thick oak expanse. The rest of her followed, carrying a tea tray laden with sandwiches and a silver pot. While sorting through old newspapers and throwing out ideas for a new story by Pyloria Braithwaite, the two young women had lost track of time.

"I knew you'd be in here! Never such a pair of bookworms have I seen!" Mrs. Basset smiled fondly at the two bright young friends who had livened up Timberly on occasion when they came to visit her employers. "I took it upon myself to bring you tea on a tray here. Her ladyship is still with Miss Julie. Oh I do keep forgetting she's Mrs. Ashford. Although now, of course, who's to say it makes any difference at all," said Mrs. Basset, shaking her head. "And Mr. Pendleton's gone off for a walk in all the mud and muck. I think the police gave him a bit of a going over, the poor fellow," she said conspiratorially. "Lord Hemming's holed up with his orchids, and Dr. Witting was waiting on Miss Julie, so he took his tea up there with her and her ladyship. I knew you'd be happier in here, so I said to Mr. Jennings I'll take their tea in, and they'll be comfortable just the two of them. A household with murders is no place for two nice young ladies, and I know you've only been picking at your meals, but you can be comfortable just the two of you, and I won't be counting the sandwiches when you send the tray back!"

With sudden pangs of hunger, the two young damsels fell with much unladylike gusto upon the delicate cucumber sandwiches, hearty pound cake, and freshly brewed tea Mrs. Basset had poured for them.

"Oh you do know the way to a girl's heart! I can see your time at that school didn't go to waste!" exclaimed Maude.

Mrs. Basset smiled, her eyes crinkling up as she thought about her five years at a girls' boarding school at the beginning of her career. "Go on, now. I just like to see you enjoying those sandwiches instead of doing whatever it is you're doing in here."

"We're just looking through some old newspapers, Mrs. Basset. Finding some interesting stories and things, you know. Just gossip really. Do you know anything of a Mrs. Hattison or a Mrs. Garfield? We've just been reading their obituaries."

Mrs. Basset shook her head at the morbid things girls got up to these days and wondered why these pretty young things should be sitting inside filling their heads with old news stories and obituaries at that. But the pull of Gossip was too difficult to resist. It was a little-known fact that Mrs. Basset subscribed to some of the more indiscreet papers, dedicatedly followed all the social news, and mined the obituaries for meaty bits of news. She always met her friend, Mrs. Tweedy, on her Thursday out to exchange their theories on who ran away with whom, and why so-and-so couldn't attend a funeral or a wedding. As Mrs. Tweedy was the vicar's housekeeper and Mrs. Basset, as housekeeper at Timberly, had doings with everyone from the butcher to the grocer's boy, these mutually informative sessions always proved to be extremely satisfactory.

Clasping her hands together, she mulled over the two names. "Hattison and Garfield? Oh! I do remember—them as left the doctor a pot of money? They were friends, you know. Not much family between the two of them, and what one did, the other did too. Bred dogs, I think. One of them has a son, and the other had a granddaughter somewhere— maybe in America. But nobody except each other really." Mrs. Basset's button eyes gleamed a little. "I did hear—I shouldn't say it, of course, the doctor being a very nice man, and very considerate for Miss Julie and her ladyship with this trouble, but there was a bit of nasty talk around the time they both died, you know. It's a while ago now, and of course I shouldn't repeat village gossip—" Mrs. Basset paused with a show of leaving Maude and Lucy to their tea. She was rewarded with eager calls for more information, and even an invitation to help herself to a jam biscuit. Not going so far as to accept this invitation—although she appreciated the friendly offer—Mrs. Basset unbent and started off on a most interesting story, much embellished and highly adorned.

To hear her tell it, both ladies had died mysteriously, and there was some upset about their wills. Although the doctor had sworn both had been in extremely poor health, their housekeepers and maids had told a different story. Why, just the week before she passed, poor Mrs. Garfield had been telling the gardener what types of runner beans she wanted planted, and how to go about caring for the roses. Always telling everyone how to do their jobs, she was. But never would her maid, who happened to be the niece of Mrs. Tweedy's friend Sarah Bark, have thought that just a few days later Mrs. Garfield would keel over at the dinner table, right in the middle of her soup! Dr. Witting did say as how she had a weak heart all along, but surely that couldn't have been the case for Mrs. Hattison. She who bred cocker spaniels and was rushing about after them all day, here and there—for they were forever getting under one's feet. Mrs. Basset shook her head and said direly that some thought Mrs. Hattison had died of a broken heart for her dear friend. But why should a woman who had happily buried three husbands die of a broken heart for a friend, pray? And oh, both very well off indeed! Dr. Witting must have been a really kind doctor—or a truly lucky one—to have patients who had both made over hefty portions of their estates to him in their last months. Mrs. Hattison's son did kick up a bit of fuss, but it all turned out quite alright, no matter what busybodies might say—Mrs. Basset cast a censorious look at the sandwiches, as though to accuse Cook—and nothing ever did come of that bottle of tonic Mr. Hattison had made such a noise about.

From there Mrs. Basset went on to more tales about Mr. Hattison, who had been a little hellion when he was a child, and had run away with the butcher's daughter to boot. Here followed a highly colorful account of this escapade, and Lucy, who had been surreptitiously taking notes the whole time, was delighted at the wealth of detail Mrs. Basset seemed to possess. She even had the good fortune to be distantly related to the seamstress who had hastily prepared a wedding dress for the brazen young hussy, and therefore knew she had been no better than she should be. Although now they were quite respectable and owned a nice little garage down by Rumsby and had two boys and a girl.

Unfortunately, just as Mrs. Basset seemed about to launch into further riveting stories about the hapless Hattison clan (who had the misfortune to be beset with any number of Mrs. Basset's gossipy acquaintances and far relations), Jennings appeared, ostensibly to take the tea tray away. Recalled by his stern gaze to her position and her duties, Mrs. Basset immediately stopped up her flow of lively gossip. She wished the two young ladies a good day and departed with the tea tray and the reproachful Jennings.

"Phew! Who would've thought the old Basset was a gossip hound!" exclaimed Maude, her curls bouncing around her head as she shook her head in wonder. Turning to see Lucy's frowning face, she asked, "What is it, old thing?"

Lucy was shuffling through the notes she had been taking as Mrs. Basset talked. "You know, Maudie, this doesn't look too good for Harris, does it?"

"Harris? Why ever? Oh the gossip she was giving us about his patients? What's that got to do with anything?"

"No, it's just...he always comes across as pure as the driven snow, doesn't he? Boring old Harris, just plodding along, doing no wrong, healing the sick, etc., etc. But it almost sounded like—I mean, he couldn't, of course, but it did sound like she was saying there was something suspicious about the two old ladies' deaths."

"Oh Luce! As if Harris ever would. He's too staid to kill even a cockroach, forget about killing patients for filthy lucre! Besides, she said it was just the son kicking up a fuss— probably because his mother didn't leave him a penny just to spite him for marrying a hussy from the butcher's shop—the meanie."

Lucy nodded absently, still staring at her notebook. "You must be right. And yet he couldn't have killed Reginald, could he?"

Maude opened her eyes wide. Usually when it came to real life Lucy was as practical and grounded as a stone. And here was Lucy questioning whether a respectable doctor—and Maude's erstwhile suitor at that—was a murderer.

"You're stark raving mad, Luce! What would he want to go kill Reginald for? Even if he did kill those two old ladies— and mind you, that's as ridiculous as it sounds—what could he gain from killing Reginald? He wasn't the old stinker's doctor, and if Reginald made such a fuss about leaving money to his own granddaughter, I hardly think he'd be inclined to leave it all to an unrelated medico."

"But you know what Reginald was like. What if he found out? Had some evidence, I mean. Maybe he was turning the screw."

"For what? I mean to say—neither of them had anything to gain from the other! If Harris didn't have anything to gain from Reginald, Reginald certainly didn't have anything to gain from Harris. What's a poor country doctor got anyway? Besides, I'm sure he wouldn't have wanted anything to happen to Harris. The man's his—was his—tenant after all. You don't go around putting the screw on your paying tenants, do you?"

"No..." Lucy looked unconvinced.

"Besides," Maude said triumphantly, "he didn't have the sliver of a chance anyway!"

At this Lucy raised her head and looked steadily at Maude. She said slowly, "You're right of course. He couldn't have done it."

"And from what Jennings was muttering on about with the footman earlier when I was coming down from my room, it seems like Garth stayed up chatting with Arthur last night—not Harris."

Lucy had lowered her head again and started folding up the newspapers she had been rifling through. "Yes, of course. But for all he can be a snake, and I do think Arthur capable of poisoning someone, you can't see him bashing someone's head in, can you?"

"And you can Harris?"

"No. No, of course not." Lucy rose from her seat and walked slowly toward the door. "Do you know, Maude, I think I am getting a bit of a headache. Just going to go up to my room for a bit. Don't mind me—it's just thinking about all these things that can't possibly be true is making me feel a bit sick in the head!"

"Luce, what is it? You're keeping something from me." Maude stood up too, looking worried.

"Nothing, Maude. I kept a copy of our list in my desk, didn't I? I'm just going to go look at it again. See if we missed anything. It's just somehow I can't quite bear to think of Arthur having committed two murders, but then I can't bear to think it of any of us. Unfortunately there's not some convenient robber or burglar we can blame, is there?" And so saying, Lucy opened the door and slipped out, leaving Maude to gaze at the blank door with a look of deep concern.

# ARREST

"Maude—how pleasant to see you here!" Rex Harte's eyes lit up in pleasure as the diminutive figure made her way toward him through the little pathways of the rose garden. Maude wore an airy yellow chiffon dress with a little grey belt. Her peach cheeks accentuated by sharp cheekbones had a rosy hue to them, and he saw an answering spark in her large eyes.

"Well, I rather thought I saw you out here and so I thought I'd just come by, you know." The artless honesty of this statement brought a smile to the inspector's lips. His bright blue eyes sparkled in response to the warmth in hers. Maude's lips rose at the corners and she fell into step beside him. Her footsteps easily found the rhythm of his, and she thought nothing further about telling him so guilelessly that she had immediately turned to meet him when she had seen him in the garden. She had felt quite naturally pulled to the same grounds he was treading. Surely there could be no harm in telling him so—it was only the truth after all. And why shouldn't she walk for a moment with an eminently respectable officer of the law?

Maude tucked a confiding hand into his arm and started walking beside him. "Have you come out here to shake the cobwebs out? Luce does that too when she—well never mind—she does it too. Takes walks I mean. In fact, I was out looking for her because she left with a bit of a headache and I didn't find her in her room. Perhaps she's on the terrace though."

"And here I thought you were out here for the pleasure of my company!" Sergeant Maddock's eyes would have bugged out of his head had he been there to witness this flirtatious sally. Of course he was not there, and so the two young people continued in this fashion for a while until a chance phrase brought Maude's attention back to the matter at hand.

"No but Rex, do listen. Lucy got the funniest idea. It was all because we were plowing through some old newspapers in the library."

"Oh?" Rex Harte experienced an uncomfortable moment as he contemplated this rather forbidding sounding hobby in one with whom, he realized, he was quickly becoming besotted. Treading cautiously, he went on, "Did you read anything interesting?"

"But that's just what I'm telling you! We were going through those fusty papers—" Harte's heart lightened again at this description "—and we came across some stories of those two women Garth had been talking about. Just yesterday—imagine! I must say, for all he was a painter, he didn't seem to talk about much besides everyday gossip. But perhaps I shouldn't say things like that—the man's dead after all." Maude peeped up at Rex through long lashes, hoping against hope he wouldn't come up with some stuffy rejoinder.

"And why pray tell should a fellow's personality change merely because he's due to dwell six feet under?"

This suitably irreverent response brought forth an enchanting dimple and Maude continued. "In any case, we just came across these obituaries of the two women, you know. Anyway, Mrs. Basset came in just then with our tea—she's an old dear really—and started gossiping nineteen to the dozen—you can't imagine!" Harte, who had not been privileged to sit through Sergeant Maddock's tea with the servants was happy to believe the sweet young lady whose eyes sparkled so brilliantly. He averred that indeed he could not imagine, and proceeded to lead her down yet another rose-lined path.

"Anyway, she started telling us all about how these two old ladies—rather harmless sounding, to be honest—were both under Harris' care, and how they'd both left him gobs of cash. Of course that started Lucy haring off thinking he's the one who bashed in poor Garth's head! She's a bit imaginative after all, but I did think I should inquire—could it have been him?"

Harte, still clasping the warm little hand, but with a graver look on his face now, paused mid-step. "I really shouldn't be discussing this with you." As the large blue-grey eyes continued looking up at him through the thick, long lashes, he heard himself saying, "But I will tell you this. Whoever it was who killed Reginald is the likeliest person to have killed Garth as well. And at the moment there isn't anybody who has a better motive for either of those than Arthur Pendleton." At the look of consternation in Maude's eyes, he continued quickly, "We're not ruling out anything yet, of course. But I'm waiting for the results from the fingerprints men and the medical examiner. Once we know what the murder weapon was and whether there were any prints, we'll have a better sense of what we're up against."

"You think he would have left prints?"

Harte sighed, shaking loose Maude's hand, which was rather strongly crushing the delicate fibers of his suit, and took it in his. "I doubt it. But perhaps he might have been too clever. And if that's the case, we'll know what's what. Everyone's got to slip up sometime."

"I suppose there wasn't anything in the papers in Reginald's room that could give you a clue?"

"Papers?"

"Didn't Lucy tell you? She's usually so good at describing things. There were a few papers strewn about. I thought you would know."

"She might have mentioned them."

"So nothing in them?"

Harte smiled with good humor. "I can't quite say, you know. It's highly irregular to talk to a witness like this!"

Beyond that he refused to say anymore, so Maude decided it would be prudent to inquire about other unconnected things such as, for example, if Rex had any siblings. A pleasant half hour passed in the recounting of his two nephews' shenanigans and the pleasures available at his sister's house in Little Bixby. It was only the lengthening shadows that recalled them both to the time. Glancing at Rex's watch, Maude let out a hearty squawk and was happy to see that he seemed unperturbed by this display of unladylike behavior. In fact, the squawk seemed to inspire him to take her into his arms and she, forgetting the necessities of her pre-dinner toilette, decided it was quite acceptable for a young lady to snuggle up to an upstanding young CID man, particularly as his embraces were accompanied by whispered sweet nothings. They parted finally with an unspoken understanding, Maude rushing upstairs to dress for dinner and Rex to find his sergeant and explain how he had come to while away the better part of an hour.

*

"Maddock! I've been looking for you. Find out if there were any papers at the scene of the crime, will you? Lord Timberly, not Ashford. I don't recall seeing them in the photographs, but Miss Grimsworth said there were a few."

"Yes, sir. And the men just called, sir. I've got my notes right here—they've found the murder weapon."

"Well? Get on with it, man!"

Sergeant Maddock, puffing his chest out, started with great dramatic flair, "Nothing on the fire irons sir, and nothing on anything else as might set off any alarms neither as you might say!"

"Might I, Sergeant? Do refrain from telling me what else they didn't find fingerprints on!"

Loath to be cut out of his delivery, Sergeant Maddock, who took a lively interest in his local theater, went on. "The fingerprints men combed the room, sir. And nary a print did they find, except," Maddock paused dramatically, "—on the murder weapon!"

"In-deed, Sergeant?"

This time the sergeant took note of the ice in the inspector's voice and decided it was time to deliver the grand finale. "The twenty year Scotch!"

Sadly the sergeant's performance went unappreciated, and Harte merely glowered at him from under his black brows, waiting for more details. Maddock continued hurriedly, "It's the same as what those two sat up drinking, sir. And neatly stowed back into the bar cart it was. Wouldn't've found it if not for a bit o' hair stickin' on the bottom of it."

"Prints?"

"Yes sir, the dead gentleman's and Arthur Pendleton's!"

\*

Breakfast at Timberly was turning out to be just as awkward and maudlin as the previous night's dinner had been. At least, Maude thought, nobody was even making a pretense of being polite or normal any more. After they had each had two slices of toast—Maude's liberally spread with marmalade and Lucy's with mulberry jam—the two slipped out and retired to the library. This was quickly becoming their preferred haunt, its murderous history notwithstanding. The fact that everyone else seemed to avoid it like the plague made it quite the best place to avoid suspicious stares and awkward conversation.

Lucy gravitated to the newspapers they had taken out the previous afternoon and Maude joined her by the table, where she spread out one of them.

Idly starting to fold up one of the newspapers, Maude asked, "Any ideas?"

"A few too many, Maudie. I'm all jumbled up." Looking up, Lucy asked straightly, "Did Harte tell you anything?"

A telltale blush rose up on Maude's cheeks, transforming her prominent features into shy prettiness, but she played with a corner of the paper and stayed silent.

"I saw you both in the rose garden, you goop. Has he proposed yet? And when are you going to meet the family?

Do I have to start playing the role of chaperone?"

"Oh Luce! Don't be a beast. Do let it go."

Hiding a smile, Lucy went back to her original question. "Well alright, I won't press, but you have to share whatever the handsome CID man has told you. It's only fair, and I promise not to pester you about him."

Maude shook her head and rolled her eyes at her friend but answered, "Nothing! Well, that's not totally true. But from whatever he said it doesn't look too good for Arthur. It almost sounded like they're just waiting for the prints to come back. And he did say Arthur has the best motive. He's one of the people who had the most to gain from Reginald's death."

"I thought he was rolling in it from the lingerie business! Isn't that what you heard?"

At this Maude had to smirk. "Imagine! We can't even make fun—and it's such a gem! But no. Rex—Inspector Harte—didn't go into any detail. He can't really say much, you know. But it didn't look good for Arthur."

"I think I should talk to him. Do you suppose he's here by now?" And Lucy, suiting her actions to her words, turned to the door, leaving Maude with a question forming upon her lips about just what exactly Lucy was going to say to the inspector.

\*

The door opened to Julie's anguished cry of "No!" and Lucy, who already had one foot out of the library, ran out to the hall without a backward glance. Maude, hastily tossing the papers aside, rushed out a step behind Lucy to find a scene that would have been comical had it not been so abjectly horrid.

In the drawing room, Arthur was standing by the fireplace clasping the mantle with one hand, his knuckles white and his face bleak. Gone was the debonair look, only to be replaced with one almost of resignation. Julie was sprawled across his chest, looking as though she was defending him with her own body from an onslaught of bullets. Her eyes wild and wide, she was blubbering after her initial heart-wrenching "No!" Marty and Biff stood to one side of the tableau as though frozen in place by a witch's spell. Harris, trying to efface himself in the curtains, appeared highly self-conscious and out of place. Judging by the flush that had mounted on his usually sedate face, he was also extremely aware of his awkward position in a dramatic episode that did not concern him.

Detective Inspector Harte, the ostensible author of this entire farcical scene, stood looking calmly at Arthur, while Sergeant Maddock had taken up a position by the door, presumably to prevent anyone escaping, although he did allow Lucy and Maude to enter.

"I'm afraid we just want to take you down to the station to get a few more matters straightened out, Mr. Pendleton. Mrs. Ashford, there is no need to take on so. I assure you nothing will happen to Mr. Pendleton."

Arthur replied in a pallid voice, "Need I ask Sir Jellaby to wait upon me, sir? I understand he is staying at the same inn as you are—perhaps you would be so kind as to let him know I shall have need of his services."

Julie interrupted him. "It was me, Inspector. I did it—you know it. This is just a ploy to get me to confess. Well I shall confess. I can't stand by and see an innocent person arrested for my crimes." Tossing her head, she made a valiant effort to bring back her usual languor. "I must admit, I thought I would get away with it, but I can't possibly let you arrest the wrong man—you must see that."

Arthur laid a hand on her shoulder and said in a brittle voice, "Do stop being a fool, Julie. Charming as it is, I assure you there is no need to throw yourself on the train tracks for me. I shan't come to any harm. They can't lay it against me—they have no proof." Putting her aside, he stepped forward and said to Harte, "I'm happy to come with you, Inspector. Am I under arrest?"

Harte, having caught Maude's glaring eye, looked back at Arthur carefully withholding any expression from his voice. "No..."

A faint smile played upon Arthur's lips, though they remained pale. With a dry undertone to his voice he said, "Not yet. Very well." At which point Julie, who had given up all pretense of being a bereaved widow, promptly gave what could only be described as a shriek and collapsed in a delicate heap on the floor.

# THE WRITER

Lucy's narrow fingers, astonishingly delicate in comparison to the rest of her sturdy form, folded, unfolded, and refolded the flimsy piece of note paper. The creases were already worn thin from her worrying at them, and the four quarters were almost coming apart. She sat with the corner of her lip caught up between her teeth, her brow furrowed, and her gaze fixed unseeingly out of the window on the wispy remnants of the weekend's cloudburst. She had sat in this exact pose folding and unfolding for a good thirty minutes. No matter how she put it, she couldn't get around it.

There were excellent reasons why Arthur should be the murderer. Murderer. The word made her cringe just to think about it. To imagine the perfectly dressed, slick Arthur dropping rat poison into a glass of Fernet and handing it to the unsuspecting, irascible Reginald, knowing full well the horror it would put his godfather through. To think of Arthur rolling up his sleeves, slipping behind Garth and bashing him with—with something blunt and wieldable. Unimaginable, really. But Arthur did have the perfect motive, the perfect opportunity, and maybe he managed to get the rat poison somehow. But there was a glitch. It wasn't really the perfect motive was it? Not if the servants' gossip about Arthur owning a lingerie business and being a well-to-do businessman, even if highly embarrassing, were true. Even if Arthur had poisoned his godfather—who, Lucy mused, seemed to be one of the few people for whom Arthur had ever expressed any affection or really any feeling—when would he have taken the rat poison? He had had no chance to enter the conservatory the whole evening prior to his visit to Reginald's room with the Fernet Branca. While Julie was blubbering it had come out that he had gone into the conservatory, but only after he came back down, to talk to her after Julie and Garth's argument. So unless he was wandering around with rat poison in his pocket the whole time, where, when, and how did he get it?

Again Lucy folded the paper. The top split, and one quarter started breaking apart from the others.

She could more easily imagine Arthur killing Garth. After all, it wouldn't be the first time a passionate young man had killed the trickster husband of his one true love. If one could only wrap one's head around the cool and collected Arthur being in love with the flighty and dramatic Julie, Lucy thought waspishly. Even as the words entered her mind, Lucy scoffed at herself, but quickly became grave again. There was another point she kept coming up against. She could easily imagine Arthur's use of poison and Arthur's desire to kill Garth (Julie's unsuitability for Arthur notwithstanding). But it was almost impossible to see Arthur killing Reginald in particular or Arthur committing such an act of brutal violence against Garth—or anyone for that matter. The finicky, almost fastidious attention to his clothes and appearance didn't play well with the image of him as a head-bashing murderer. In fact, Lucy was quite sure Arthur would hesitate to even approach anyone bleeding to death to offer assistance lest his suede gloves should get a drop on them. So if Arthur wouldn't kill Reginald and if he wouldn't brain anybody, the crimes didn't fit him. The person didn't match the *modus operandi*, as the crime books called it.

Lucy sighed. She was going about this all wrong, of course. Inspector Harte would be much more methodical, using hard evidence instead of hard-to-prove convictions. She opened the sheet of paper again. In addition to her own assessment of Arthur's innocence, this was the only thing she could think of that might help her to find a clue. She and Maude had made the list of suspects and laughingly included themselves on it without actually grasping what they had been talking about. In the back of her mind Lucy had had the comfortable belief that it would all get sorted out and Harte would easily arrest some interloper whom none of them had previously known about. An escaped prisoner, perhaps. Or a madman. Garth's death and Arthur's arrest had changed that sanguine belief. Even as she knew Harte was right—all the hard evidence pointed to Arthur—she couldn't help but think that he—and she—had missed something vital on the little list in her hands.

The paper finally tore, unable to withstand the constant assault of her fingers, and came apart in two even halves. As they fell into each hand, Lucy's eyes lit up. Something about the physical tearing of the paper had realigned some ideas where previously they had been jumbled up. Feverishly, she straightened the two pieces of paper and laid them side-by-side again. Hands shaking, she carefully smoothed them on the little knee-hole desk at which she sat. She threw her mind back over the events of the past two days, trying to remember in minute detail everything that had happened, that had been seen, that had been said. It was impossible to believe, and yet, if it was true, it had been staring them in the face the entire time. She had to go find Inspector Harte immediately. He was about to make a grave mistake.

Lucy flung the door open and dashed out of her room, the paper halves floating behind her, one part floating out to the landing, the other coming gently to rest just inside her doorway. As she hurried down the steps, hoping to catch at least Sergeant Maddock in the library, she didn't look behind her or realize she had left her bedroom door open with the little torn list lying across the threshold.

\*

Not finding either Sergeant Maddock or Inspector Harte in the library, Lucy paused for an instant to think things over. Of course Inspector Harte had taken Arthur to the village—

not under arrest, but with the strict understanding that he was not to leave police custody, which Lucy considered to be not much different. Julie, after recovering from her swooning spell, had gone after him despite his (almost bored, Lucy thought) protestations that he did not require her support. Lucy had imagined a little vaguely that Sergeant Maddock would have remained behind, but realized he must have gone down to the police station as well. After all, they had their murderer. Why would he stay on?

Suddenly, she became aware of just how quiet the house was. It was still a little while before lunch, so all the servants were downstairs having their own meal. Even Jennings had retired to his pantry, and one of the footmen would be keeping an ear peeled for the bell to sound notifying him someone was at the door. Feeling a little frisson run down her back, Lucy gave herself a sound shake, telling herself there was no need to turn into a quivering rabbit just because she couldn't see anyone else around. Maude had to be either curled up with a book somewhere in the house or walking in the gardens. It was pleasant in the late morning now the rain had gone, taking the pent up humidity with it, and the ground had dried a bit.

Wondering where Marty, Biff, and Harris were, Lucy made her way to the morning room to look for Maude. Not finding her in there, she turned, and as she did so, thought she saw some movement in the conservatory. Maude must have gone in to look at the orchids again. Maybe she was sketching them, thought Lucy. Maude sometimes made illustrations to go with Lucy's stories and had a neat hand when it came to sketching. Making her way toward the conservatory, Lucy bumped into a marble-topped wooden table and gave a start that almost knocked a little bowl of peonies off. She steadied the brass bowl and placed her hand palm down on the smooth, cold surface to steady herself. The little frisson was turning into a severe case of jumpiness, and Lucy knew she'd be better off with Maude. Talking through her theory would make her see if it actually made sense or not, and if it did, maybe the two of them could rouse up their chauffeur to go into town to get Harte and explain everything. Wandering around the seemingly empty house wasn't doing her nerves any favors, so Lucy continued over to the conservatory and went in, confident she'd find Maude taking the proportion of an orchid petal with one eye screwed close and her tongue sticking out.

\*

Harte looked up from the notes spread out on the desk in front of him and directed his sharp gaze at the frightened, obstinate young woman in front of him.

"I have your statement, taken after your grandfather's death, here. I just want to go over it once again with you. Could you tell me in detail about the cocktail hour?"

"I—I've already told you. I gave the coffee to my grandfather."

"I understand that. I'm just asking you to go over the entire cocktail hour, if you don't mind."

"Why? Can't you see? That's when I did it! That's when I put the poison in!"

"And when did you get the poison from the conservatory?"

"I—I went into the conservatory to talk to Garth!"

"That was later in the evening, was it not? After your grandfather had retired to bed?"

Arthur had wandered over to the window and lit a cigarette, but at this he turned and said harshly, "Do stop being a fool, Julie. There really isn't any need for you to play the martyr here. Apart from the fact that it's not actually doing me any favors, Harte isn't about to believe you killed your grandfather even if you lie till you're blue in the face. Just tell him what he's asking. I have a suspicion—" and at this Arthur looked at the inspector with a bland smile, "—that he isn't asking these questions for the sake of entertainment." Arthur stubbed out his cigarette and came to sit down at the table next to Julie, facing Harte with confidence.

They had been at it for over half an hour now, and the little room Harte had taken over in the local police station was starting to get stuffy and claustrophobic. The sparse furnishings were none too comfortable, and Harte was growing more and more concerned with Pendleton's assured air. He wondered if his questions had given anything away, but acknowledged that somehow he couldn't quite fit Arthur Pendleton into the role of murderer. Besides which, he had spent the past thirty minutes closely observing Julie and Arthur's interactions, and somehow the role of lovers didn't quite jump to mind. Julie seemed to have transferred her affections rather abruptly from Ashford to Pendleton. However, it was quickly becoming evident Pendleton himself was rather less than charmed by this change.

The inspector gave a little bow and spoke warmly to Julie. "Mrs. Ashford—Julie, if you prefer—Mr. Pendleton is correct. I don't believe you had anything to do with either murder. I merely want to ascertain a chain of events. And to set your mind at ease, I am not sure I find the idea of Mr. Pendleton as chief murder suspect to be especially attractive either. Would you please describe the cocktail hour in detail? Begin with who was there when you entered, and who came in after you, please."

Julie's shoulders relaxed slightly and she leaned back against the hard wooden chair back. She seemed a little bewildered. The others in the room looked equally confused, regarding the inspector in bemused expectation. Only Arthur sat forward, looking alertly at the inspector. With a deep breath, Julie started describing the evening again.

\*

The conservatory was peaceful and charming, Lucy thought, as she stepped in through the open door. But impossible to see around the huge palm to the rest of the indoor garden. If Maude was sitting there, she couldn't see her immediately. There was a comfortable wooden bench a little farther in with a good view of the orchids—maybe she was there.

"Maudie? Are you in here? I've been looking for you everywhere! I have something to tell you. I think we've all been hideously wrong!"

Hearing a rustle, Lucy walked farther into the conservatory, pushing aside a branch as she did so, and came to a sudden stop. She watched the figure approach her as though she were entranced.

"Would you rather tell it to me instead?"

# CONVERSATION IN THE CONSERVATORY

Harris Witting stood before Lucy, wearing a pair of gardening gloves and holding a pair of long gardening shears.

"Hello Lucy. How are you? Pleasant in here, isn't it? I thought I'd help Biff out by trimming this little orange tree. That branch is rather overgrown. I noticed it the other day."

"How—how kind of you. You haven't seen Maude, have you? She was supposed to meet me in the conservatory at—n-now."

Lucy couldn't draw her eyes away from Harris and his large gloved hands holding the heavy shears. Her voice sounded tinny in her ears as the blood rushed to her head, pounding and drowning out any other sounds. There was no real reason to be afraid, only she had never seen Harris' eyes looking so much like cold, hard iron. And it had never occurred to her that the fellow she usually dismissed as dull and stolid was powerful enough to knock down a door. Her mind flitted back up the stairs to the little torn piece of paper and she couldn't help but raise one hand slowly to her throat, the other clutching at her skirt and crushing the soft cotton material. Unwillingly her thoughts went back to that fateful morning and lingered on Harris, how she had thought his training as a doctor allowed him to be so calm in the face of such a horrible scene, one which had even made the usually cool and urbane Arthur's blood drain from his face. How he had calmly examined Reginald and pronounced him dead. How he had been the only one to approach the body, as the rest couldn't even bear to look. How he had been the first to go to Garth. Lucy had replayed that morning a hundred times in her mind. Had Jennings ever said Garth was murdered? Or just that he was dead? Had either he or Biff said Garth was in the library? She gave a start as Harris started speaking again. Was his voice always this inflectionless? Were his eyes always this cold?

"How nice. I haven't seen her downstairs, have you? In fact, I didn't see anybody else around." Harris looked around a little theatrically. "I thought Marty and Biff went off with Julie to try and save the unfortunate Arthur."

Lucy's heart dropped when she heard Marty and Biff were down in the little village. "Oh—she must be on her way. I'm sure of it. Maybe she's waiting out in the hall. I'll just check, shall I?" Lucy started backing away from Harris, but was arrested by his next words.

"Aren't you going to ask me when I saw the overgrown branch, Lucy? When I didn't have a chance to come into the conservatory at all?"

She didn't want to know. The words chilled her to the bone, but she tried to play them off lightheartedly. "Oh it never even occurred to me! I suppose you must have come in some other time. Would you like to come with me? I'm sure Maude is waiting for me outside—maybe we can all take a walk in the gardens together. I—I know she must be waiting for me."

"Please, sit down, Lucy." The doctor's voice had dropped until it was almost a whisper. "I think we need to have a chat."

*

Arthur, Julie, Biff, and Marty were in conference with the long-suffering Jellaby in a little room off the inspector's makeshift office in the local station. Harte was standing at the ancient pockmarked desk, his brows knitted over the printed sheet of paper in his hand. "Maddock—see what you make of this, will you?"

Sergeant Maddock took the papers and started reading

through the fingerprints report once again, wondering what the inspector had seen. After a few moments he looked up with a puzzled frown and handed the report back to his superior.

"The prints, sir—on the bottle. They're—there's something about it. A bit odd like, them prints being at the one side on the bottom there..."

"And not the top," Harte finished. "Now why would Arthur Pendleton, who admits he was talking with Ashford in the library and drinking Scotch—the Glenlivet 20 to be precise—with the man, not leave any prints at the top of the bottle? You'd expect to see at least a few prints on the neck—the fellow would have to open the bottle, dammit! Or even if not Pendleton's, Ashford's—or anyone else for that matter who'd had a sip in the past few days."

"He could have wiped it down, sir. After the murder. Everybody knows about fingerprints these days."

"You don't sound very convinced of that theory yourself. And I'm bound to agree with that note of doubt I hear. Even if he did upend it and use it as a blunt instrument—likely, given the trace amounts of tissue and hair the fingerprints men found on it—if he were to wipe it down, what more natural than to wipe off the entire bottle? Obviously the part that met Ashford's head has been wiped, as has the neck. So why not the rest of the bottle?"

"I can't say, sir. And about the papers you asked about— are you certain there were any? I inquired with all the local men who were first at the scene, and none of them can remember anything."

"Both Miss Grimsworth and Miss Belling told me about it, but the photographs didn't show any papers either."

Fiddling with the sheet of paper, Harte walked over to the little window and stared out at the top of Timberly Hall. It was just visible past the cottage roofs and trees. Turning, he gestured to a bedraggled sheet of paper in one corner of the desk. "Hand me that, will you? I get the feeling we've been missing something. And I've felt like it's been on that sheet of paper the whole time. And get Jellaby—I haven't had time to go over the papers he brought with him, but now's as good a time as any to take a look at them."

\*

"Oh, thank you! It's so very lovely! I'll put it in a little vase by my bed. I'm sure Marty will let me have one."

"Now there you go, miss. Late summer roses like these are meant for the likes of ye." Groby had all the gruff charm of an ancient retainer who had relinquished his most arduous tasks to younger garden "boys" but took on mild responsibilities to keep up the pretense of being head gardener. His responsibilities took the form of activities that didn't require much strain for his knees, like deadheading roses. It was a perk of his job, he had always thought, that interesting young ladies like this Miss Maude were always falling in love with his roses and were willing enough to listen to his stories in exchange for a pretty little bud or two.

"Strange doings up at the house, miss, if you don't mind me saying so. Folks have it there's one of the party that's a murdering madman. 'Twould be a pity if it turned out to be Mr. Arthur after all this hullaballoo."

"I—I'm sure—" Maude shook her head and went on with conviction in her voice, "I'm sure he didn't do it, you know. I just can't believe it of Arthur."

"Ay, there's the rub. He's a mite high in his instep, but I'll grant him he always has a kind word for me and asks after the missus. She used to be housemaid here when he was a boy and would visit the old gent, ye know. Always slipped him a lemon drop when his ma weren't around. He were right fond of the old gent, that I'll give him. Never too fond of Miss Marty—sorry, her la'ship—never can get used to seeing her married to a lord no matter how many years Lord Biff's been around! But she don't treat him with the heavy hand he needs. That's why he and the old lord got along so well. Knew they could each give as good as they got."

He leaned on his ancient wheelbarrow and chewed meditatively on the wad of tobacco tucked into his cheek. His eyes were troubled at the thought that Arthur might be arrested for Lord Reginald's murder. Maude supposed Garth's death didn't figure much in his mind.

"Well, if only they do find it was a murdering lunatic I would sleep much better at night. Although I shouldn't like to think of one being loose, I can't quite believe Biff or Harris would've done it!" Maude shuddered at the thought, though her last words didn't quite have the same conviction with which she had defended Arthur.

"His lordship? Nah! He's too soft to even drown a cat! Had to have Jimmy take off the kittens in the barn without Lord Biff knowing—he wouldn't've let it happen at all! Place'd be overrun! But that doctor there—I ain't sayin' as he's done it, but he weren't a big admirer of the old gent."

Maude looked up, startled. "Why? I mean—what do you mean? Surely—I didn't know they knew each other too well."

"Know each other! His Lordship were the doctor's landlord! And I heard from old Barney down in town, him as what does the doctor's garden, his lordship'd been making a fuss about the practice for a few months now. Been sayin' some nasty things to the doctor, cutting like, ye know. Oh no, they'd had words before up here too. I heard them going at it bellows and tongs when I were clipping some bushes over by the library just a few days ago—right when the doctor arrived here, must'a been. Going on like a couple of cats, they was. And talking 'bout a pair of bats!" Groby let out a hearty chuckle at this rhyme. Seeing Maude's confused expression he stopped to explain, "Two old biddies, ye know—them ladies what went and conked a few months ago—maybe you don't know a'cos of them being down in the town here."

Maude let out a gasp as she cut her finger on a thorn. She hadn't even realized she had clenched her fist. "Groby—you—you don't mean Mrs. Hattison do you? And Garfield?"

Scratching his head, Groby considered and said after an excruciating pause, "That's them a'right, miss. Saved a pretty penny, both of 'em—and no one to blow it on 'cept for them dogs what they used ter breed." The next minute he was left scratching his head again as Maude ran down the path, the rosebud falling from her hand in her haste.

*

Maddock jumped up, his mustache quivering excitedly. "I've got it sir—the butler never said where the body was!"

"Are you sure, man?"

"Yes sir. And what Miss Julie said about how the doctor originally had Lord Timberly's coffee cup and she took it from him to give to her grandfather—that's done it!"

"And that damn list Maude and Lucy gave us has been telling us all along that Harris was right behind them when they were on the landing, but one of the last to arrive in the drawing room for cocktails. How could we overlook such a perfect opportunity to sneak in and get the poison? As a doctor he'd know just what the effect would be!"

"Do you think it safe sir, Miss Belling and Miss Grimsworth there alone with him? What if they show him the list and he puts two and two together?"

Harte was already reaching for his hat and rising from the desk. He had just been going over the leases Jellaby had brought with him for Lord Timberly. Harte and Maddock had also been poring over Maude and Lucy's list and finally seen the little time discrepancy for the doctor. Immediately they had moved on to the statements to find some corroboration. The two had spent the last twenty minutes riffling through the statements, and the inspector was already kicking himself for not jumping to the fact that the doctor had been the only one of the company who had had the opportunity to filch anything from the crime scene in the bedroom as well as the only one who had been alone with Garth Ashford's body in the library. Maddock's words only confirmed the suspicion that had been growing ever since Julie's recounting of the cocktail party. At that moment

Jellaby opened the door to the connecting room and entered, followed by Arthur and the rest of the Timberly party. Before he had a chance to say anything, Harte was shouting, "Call Timberly—now! Tell Maude and Lucy to stay together. Go down to the kitchen, anything. Just stay together—safety in numbers!" And in the next instant he was gone, followed by the surprisingly nimble bulk of Sergeant Maddock.

\*

"They'll know it was you. There's nobody else to blame."

"Oh I don't know." Harris opened the shears and closed them again with an evil snick. "Accidents happen, you know. Just last week I had to send a fellow up to London for a surgery because he'd tripped and fallen on his gardening shears. Patched him up as best as I could, of course, but it was almost beyond me. At the right angle, you'd be surprised how quickly a person can bleed out. Before anyone could hear your cries and come running to you." Harris took a step closer. "And of course I would come running. I should hate to have anything happen to my dear friend Lucy."

"I—I left a note."

At this Harris let out a genuinely amused chuckle. "Did you? Did you write that you were taking a stroll in the conservatory with no intention of falling on a pair of shears? And did you leave it in someone's safekeeping, and they'll send it to the inspector if you don't turn up alive within the next hour?" His mocking tone changed to a grim, harsh rasp. "I found your little scrap of paper in the doorway to your bedroom. You really should keep a closer eye on important lists, you know. I've taken the precaution of burning that up, of course, but don't think I didn't see immediately what you let slip in your little chronology. If I'd been right behind you on the stairs before dinner, where was I right after you got downstairs? Why was I the last one in? And you have a keen eye, Lucy, I'll give you that. I seemed afraid of Reginald, did I? I thought I did rather a good job keeping a straight face, actually, but I think you might have been the only one to find anything amiss."

"I gave a copy of the list to the inspector!" Lucy burst out, desperate now. Harris was too close, just a foot away. She could never outrun him. The rusted shears gleamed dully. Her mind was whirring in a million different directions and she could only hope he would believe her and realize it was folly to kill her.

Her words arrested him for a second. "When?" he barked out.

"T-two d-days ago." Lucy's lips quivered. She was almost at the end of her tether, but a little hope dawned at this. It was quickly dashed in the next instant. Her words, instead of striking fear into the doctor's heart, seemed to give him comfort. Lucy paled even further as she saw his lips turn up in a smile.

"My dear Lucy, do you actually think I would believe that? To think the inspector—a bright chap, I'll give him that—has had the list for two days and hasn't put two and two together? I'm afraid it just can't be. He would've bounded in and arrested me right off the bat, before even poor Garth had a chance to open his big mouth."

"Garth!" Lucy exclaimed. The only thought in her mind was to keep him talking long enough for—at this her thoughts ran into a blank wall. She didn't know what good would come of keeping him talking, except for the inevitable, but there it was. Maybe Maude would come down the stairs. Oh Maude, Maude, where are you! One part of Lucy's mind filled with irrational annoyance at her best friend—why wasn't she here, in her moment of need?

"Why Garth? You killed him too—why?"

"Why, because he knew I'd been talking to Reginald about those two old women, of course. I thought I'd had such luck in gathering up the letters Lord Timberly had in his room when you all couldn't stand the sight of his body. They would've provided an excellent motive for me, but I took care of them. And then along comes Garth, blabbing about the very thing I was so keen to hide. He was telling you at lunch, don't you remember? I couldn't have that getting out, you know. But if it makes you feel any better, I get the feeling Garth didn't really love Julie, nor she him either. It's a pity Julie's true love will have to go to prison instead of me, but that just can't be helped. It's not such a great loss to humanity, you know. Not Reginald either. The old rat was blackmailing me! Wanted me to give up my practice because he'd been friends with one of the old dames—though I think it was because he'd found a higher bidder for the practice, really."

Lucy let out a cry as Harris grabbed her arm, saying, "Enough talk, my dear—I can't afford to waste more time" and lunged at her with the shears.

She heard a loud crash accompanied by the tinkling of glass and the sound of a balloon popping. An excruciating pain slashed across her stomach just as something hit her head, and she wondered that she had the energy to scream so loudly. Was that animal cry coming from her own throat? With this last irrelevant thought, Lucy Belling slumped and fell with a thud to the cold tiled floor.

# EPILOGUE

"Here's your hellcat. Don't blame me if he scratches you to death. He's been a regular horror the whole day."

"Jacko!" Lucy welcomed the grumpy cat, who intuitively tried to settle on her middle. "Ow! You are a hellcat. Why would you pick that spot and that spot only, you brute?" Lucy pulled him under her arms where he deigned to settle himself and even nuzzled into her shoulder in a rare sign of affection. She was settled in her own comfortable bed with a dozen pillows propping her up. A little bell lay within arm's reach and her notebook full of the Hon. Holly's exploits lay under a dangerously uncapped pen on one of the cushions. Although she had felt able to be up and about for a week or more now, Maude and Dorcey had turned into veritable dragons at the mere suggestion, and had successfully kept her in bed by the simple expedient of taking away all her dresses and shoes.

Maude pushed a pile of papers off the seat next to her bed and sat down with a whump. "Well, that's that. She came to visit, but I managed to fend her off of coming up to see you—told her you were still too ill. I actually felt rather bad for her, poor dear."

Lucy raised her eyebrows in surprise. She knew Maude had been trying to dodge a visit from Mrs. Witting for three weeks now, ever since that horrible day in the conservatory.

Maude raised her face to Lucy, a sorrowful look in her eyes. "She never knew any of it. He was her golden boy, you know. Quite a shock to hear he was dead, and even worse, he'd killed two people that we know of and probably killed two old women as well—ones whom he'd beguiled into leaving their money to him."

Lucy was quiet, stroking Jacko and playing with the fringe of the burnt orange paisley shawl wrapped around her shoulders. "She—she didn't—she didn't blame—"

"Luce! Don't be an idiot! *He* tried to kill *you* remember? You're such a dolt. Good thing Rex took a pot shot at him, otherwise you'd've been clipped right in half by those evil shears he had out. Not that he didn't get a jolly good go at you—you're going to have a devil of a scar!"

This took away Lucy's doldrums and brought a spark back to her eyes. "Thanks! And a big bump on my head and not a few little scars all over my arm too, thanks to your idiotic trick! Tell me the truth, Maude—were you trying to brain me too? Or was that just a happy side effect?"

"I saved you, thank you very much! If I hadn't thrown that handy old brick through the window, who knows, Harris might even have got you clean through instead of just sticking the shears in part of the way! I can't quite help it if you got in the way a bit and got bunged up as well. Anyway," Maude continued, settling more cozily into her chair, "Marty called to see how you're doing and to say once again how sorry she is to have invited a murdering doctor to her weekend party, and of course she doesn't mind anymore that we ratted her and Biff out. Ooh and I have some gossip about Julie and Arthur too! I finally got the whole story out of Marty. It was last year that the two were getting closer, but apparently it was never serious for Arthur. When he told her so, Julie went off in a fit of pique and of course, we know how that ended. But now Julie's being quite a bore about Arthur again—feels he owes her something because she offered to give herself up for his crime. Although of course, since it wasn't his crime I can't blame him for running in the opposite direction, which is what Marty said he's doing right now. In any case, Julie's silliness notwithstanding, Marty and Biff are to live happily ever after without the malingering presence of Reginald Timberly. So all's well that ends well!"

"And is that all Maudie?" Lucy asked with a sly smile. She'd heard all about it from Dorcey, of course, how that nice inspector man called every day to "check on Lucy's progress," as he phrased it. "I thought I heard the 'phone ring twice today."

"Oh that!" Maude gave an elaborate sigh and said, rather inconsequently, "Little Bixby seems to be a darling little place, you know—and not too far either. Perhaps the two of us could go there sometime, once you're on your way to healing up. I believe I have an acquaintance of sorts there."

# ABOUT THE AUTHOR

Maithili Pradhan is an attorney and human rights advocate living in Brooklyn, NY with her husband. She grew up in India and the United States on a steady diet of Agatha Christies and Georgette Heyers and is a life-long aficionado of cozy mysteries. Her favorite activity is curling up with a good book, a soft blanket, and a hot cup of tea.

For updates about the next installment in the Lucy Belling and Maude Grimsworth mystery series, please visit http://www.maithilipradhan.com.

Made in the USA
Middletown, DE
11 March 2015